Marking the Magic Circle

Marking the Magic Circle

*poetry, fiction, and essays
by George Venn*

with photographs by Jan Boles

Oregon State University Press
Corvallis, Oregon

Other books by George Venn

Sunday Afternoon: Grande Ronde (Prescott St. Press, 1976)
Off The Main Road (Prescott St. Press, 1978)

Photo on cover and pages i and v by Bernard L. Thomas

The paper in this book meets the guidelines for permanence and durability of the Committee on Production Guidelines for Book Longevity of the Council on Library Resources and the minimum requirements of the American National Standard for Permanence of Paper for Printed Library Materials 239.48-1984.

Library of Congress Cataloging-in-Publication Data
Venn, George, 1943-
    Marking the magic circle.

    1. Oregon—Literary collections. I. Title.
PS3572,E48M3   1987   818'.5409   86-19185
ISBN 0-87071-352-3 (alk. paper)

For my parents
Ernest Fyfe, Beth Alice Mayo, Frank A. Venn

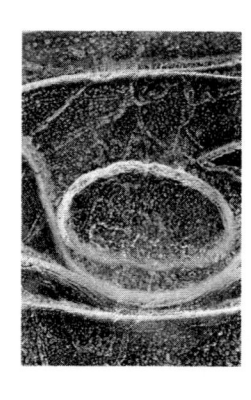

Contents

～

A Note To the Reader

This book presents you with a collage. It defies an obvious linear or chapter-by-chapter progression, but becomes coherent when viewed as a cyclic arrangement—images of places. This book also presents you with a motet. The contrapuntal voices of the poet, essayist, and storyteller appear to be singing different songs, but they are all actually singing one polyphonous, polytonal mass. Finally, this book presents you with a wilderness settlement: seven homesteads in a valley. They always work together, but remain somewhat distant from each other.

Those metaphors for a book may still leave you wondering about *Marking The Magic Circle.* "What is this all about?" you may shout outside my window late some night. You may remind me that the medium here is not pasticcio, a choir, or settlers. It is language. Unlike visual art, music, and frontiers, language is traditionally used for making a clear, unavoidably linear progression with a definite beginning, middle, and end. You won't find that kind of *linear arrangement* here. However, that doesn't mean there is no unity in cyclic, recursive form.

My theme is stated in the title essay, the first essay in the book but the last essay to be written, and I repeat that thematic statement in all the other sections:

a region is a microcosm—a magic circle centered on *home.* The values generated by that circle are many, but I have limited myself here to three—confidence, wholeness, intimacy. For me, the authentic map of the universe is composed of these microcosms—domes and domes of specific human light, crossing all abstract political, geographic, economic, and racial boundaries.

That theme develops in the first section by counterpoint: the first affirmative essay is contrasted with a subsequent poem and story which show how a child's confidence, wholeness, and intimacy can be threatened by the devoutly religious people who share his magic circle. The last poem in the section restates the theme of the opening essay.

The other six sections are six other possible places: school, rural county, northwest, Changsha, small town, farm. In each of them, the voices explore what happens to the values I've ascribed to the magic circle. The other sections follow this same general pattern—statement/counterstatement—but not always in that same order or proportion found in the first section. Like the motet, the voices in each chapter repeat the theme of the title essay, then use the new locale to develop new variations on that theme. Like the collage, the sections may seem disparate, but images recur. Like the seven homesteads in the valley, the seven sections are all sweating out the paradoxes that haunt any human frontier.

Places, voices, point, and counter, how many are hiding in the center? You will see.

George Venn
La Grande, Oregon
November 1986

Acknowledgments

This collage, which collects about one-third of the prose and poetry I've attempted during the last ten years, also represents the encouragement, good will, and affection of many people who are not named herein, but without whom most of this would not have been written.

I want to thank my extended family—Boettchers, Chapmans, Falcks, Fyfes, Gemmells, Mayos, Purdys, Sanders, Smiths, Van Eatons, Walshes—where I owe a large and conspicuous debt for hospitality and good will since 1943.

To my teachers in general and to these language teachers in particular—Mrs. Dahl at Spirit Lake High School and Dr. Louie Attebery at The College of Idaho, as well as H. G. Merriam, Bill Kittredge, Earl Ganz, Madeline De Frees, and others on the graduate faculty at the University of Montana—I owe direct and specific thanks for nurturing my relationship with my own language and experience and so not making me into a simple extension of themselves.

To the Oregon Committee for the Humanities, I owe thanks for their funding of the research that led to the essay on Nard Jones. Others who assisted me directly in that project include librarians Margaret Sutherland, Darcy Dauble, Jack Evans, Larry Dodd, Lee B. Webster, as well as the librarians at the Umatilla County Library in Pendleton. Also, the people in Weston who knew Nard Jones and granted me interviews, especially George Gottfried, Hugh Gilliland, Willmarth Reynaud, Cliff Price, and Wayne O'Hara, should be thanked here for their candid willingness to assist me.

In the act of translating poems from the Chinese, the work of my collaborator, Prof. Liu Pei Wu, of Changsha Railway Institute, Hunan, Peoples' Republic of China, was invaluable, as were the assistance of Xu Rei Fang, Daisy Rothgery, John and Yilin Moe, Anne Stephens, Darcy Dauble, Mandy Gillis, Hillary Thompson, and Suzie Sparkhall—the last three my riotous friends from the British VSO. Without them, no real translating would have been done.

Behind all of this manuscript stand three people who have encouraged me to continue as a writer—Vi Gale, poet and publisher at Prescott St. Press; Lois Barry, my colleague in Writing at Eastern Oregon State College; and Elizabeth Cheney, my wife, who has tolerated my need for solitude enough for me to finish this—but who's waiting for a novel.

Finally, the greatest credit for shaping this manuscript into its present form belongs to my congenial, patient, and loyal editor at Oregon State University Press, Jo Alexander. She has acted quickly, honestly, and decisively in all stages of this project. She recognized better than I did what my limits and strengths were, pointed these out, asked for revisions, and kept good faith with me during the entire two years of revising, editing, and producing this book.

For all of them, I hope that language—perhaps this volume—will be an instrument of peace and my gratitude.

Part I

Marking the Magic Circle

December night, end of the year. Late. A blizzard roars through the bare trees outside and drives freezing rain against the windows. Ice storm. On the ridge, not even the deer move from their beds in thick timber, their nostrils venting steam to the night. All public power is gone. All lines down. I go to the window to look out, but the glass is wrinkled and frozen into a sacred blur, so I return to this page by an old kerosene lamp, its three flames receding into the storm beyond the windows. Behind me, lodgepole logs shift and settle in the stove; the fire's heat surrounds my shoulders but leaves my knees and shins chilled. I listen. Blizzard subsides, then gusts, subsides, then blasts a white whirlwind past my window. The glass trembles. I am at home. The dog barks at some sound in that storm I cannot hear. "What?" I say to her. Getting up to see what she heard, I feel the old farmhouse sway like a ship.

～

This is why writing begins for me—an immediate place and moment demanding attention, inviting names, suggesting reflections, encouraging exploration. If I'm lucky, something will appear. That doesn't always happen. Maybe it won't happen here, but language does have this power to create an immediate sensible cosmos out of the blizzard—whatever it might be—and the inaudible sounds inside it.

On another night like this one, caught between personal loss and inexpressible anger, I wrote this poem and found through it some order where none seemed possible before:

Winter Sailor

Even the trees reef now.
The blizzard screams.
I sway and moan inside
ready to jump in the maw
of any whale.

Cut loose, I'm blasted
leaves wrenched north.
There on the bald ridge
light rides over snow—
something dies.

A horseman comes.
His silver bridle gleams
to me for miles. I reach
out to this plain dream
of slight new rein.

Space is organized around a sacral center . . . let us remember that not only so-called primitives but literate and sophisticated peoples are disposed to structure their worlds this way.
Yi-Fu Tuan

Back inside, I check the fire, add a round of lodgepole, then come back to this desk by the window. The lamp still gives its three receding flames to the storm. Salvaged from my grandparents' basement, the lamp's round glass base is etched with a nine-pointed star. Above the base, the round belly of lamp oil rises—incarnadine—nearly half gone. Inside that reservoir, the old wick coils like a snakeskin. I have never changed wicks—this must be my grandmother's work. The brass round chimney base sits like a dusty hat on top of the glass reservoir. From the groove in the narrowing crown, a tongue of soft yellow flame—blue centered, almost invisible—sways in the drafts of storm leaking in around the old wood casing. The glass chimney is broken and gone. On a clear cold night, you could see this lamp across the dark fields inviting you in. Tonight, it would be useless. The whiteout has come. I scrawl on.

As an old family lamp might create a center that could transform a better night, so in my own life there are centering places that give arrangement to my experience. The houses I was born into or learned to live—replete with attics, basements, hideaways, kitchens, barns, stumps, creeks, lakes, rivers, animals, plants, friends—all became centers of protection where holy facts were shown to me: love's hands and milk, strong wood walls and fires, singing and death, water and the answered cry, silence and the voices of trees, animals and light—the true edges of all things. Those sanctuaries I carry with me, always returning to them, considering them, writing about them. They are fires where cedar burns unconsumed. They are mountains where wrestling angels wait. But they were separated by miles and years, and the greatest demand of my growing up seemed to be to hold them together, to call them all one name, to see them as one. From Louie Attebery, then Harold Merriam, I learned that a river— south fork murky, north fork clear—might unify those places, those lives. I called them *Northwest*. All secrets, truths, mysteries resided there. Northwest became my dream house, my Mt. Analogue, a place to stand, a landscape of possibilities. I was at home in that space marked by the Columbia River. I had a world with many centers and a real edge—a region.

Later, I learned that people universally scribe a similar sacred circle with their lives and homes at the center, a circle with a meaningful series of concentric rings spiraling outward from that center toward an edge—an opening, a passageway to the infinite, the unknown. Though often hidden from us, that magic circle and its positions have given centuries of arrangement and expression to human lives. Saying *well-rounded, rounded out, coming full circle, come around, on the edge, on edge, edgy, far out, outcast, exorbitant, extremities, heart, core, outback, out west, eccentric,* I touched the top of the circle's linguistic mountain. In the cosmographies of 6th century B.C. China, ancient Greece, and medieval Europe, I found recurrent images of the sacred circle. In *Mental Maps* (Penguin, 1974), I learned from Gould and White that human information, understanding, and emotional involvement *decrease* with the distance from home. From my students, I also have good evidence that everyone—no matter where they moved—created a magic circle as I had with home at the center and meaningful concentric rings moving outward to the edge. "Being is round," says Bachelard. While the boundaries and centers on that internal symbolic map may change, its topography and contours are apparently archetypal.

Probably never found in the geography texts, that circle I traced around the Columbia drainage gave definition to the region where I felt I belonged. Frequently, that map becomes more concrete—the work of poems.

Early Morning:
Washington 12 Toward Ohanapecosh

Along the dammed Cowlitz River
stump ranch fields are thickening
with swampgrass and buttercups.
Blackberries are always overgrowing
cedar stumps jutting like monuments
in the pasture. Alders jump the fence
ferns move in, moss takes the shake roof
and swallows fly out the kitchen window
over mole hills and rank thistles.

I could be farming that homestead
long enough to see my own posts rot
my fences rust and disappear in floods.
I was born to this land; land is my name.
Here means my first father died,
my uncles lived, my brother played summers
away in grandfather's timothy and clover.
I know the faller's ax, pulaski, frow,
peavey, scythe, the crosscut saw.

Davis Creek, Tilton River,
Rainy Valley, Packwood, Mossyrock—
the small loggerheaded towns asleep
in the century of their own sawdust
the logging trucks aiming their reaches
like howitzers at the silent Cascades.
Sawlogs wait prisoner at the mill;
teepee burner glows like rusted hell.
Bare bulb of the yard light burns over
the yellow crummy streaked with dew.

I could be a gyppo sleeping in that shack
where the junked-out cars are full of dust.
I could be swinging out of bed on hoot owl
caulks and hard hat my only human hope.
I could be pulling green chain at the mill
packing a black lunchbucket, driving home
half-drunk from the Ashford Tavern payday.
I've chased chokers, borne off cants,
slung tongs, stickered and stacked on bunks
until I didn't know who my own hands were.

As the sun burns around the corner
I give this valley all the names I have
drive myself for higher country on Rainier—
Indian Bar, Summerland, Mystic Lake—
the alpine park no man will ever cut
where I'll camp tonight and sleep
a glacial sleep for lives I'll always be.
When I come down, no one in these towns
will know my name or consider the avalanche
of lupine melting in my hands like laws.
I'll see the second growth and death of work
then fly like a shining crow for the river.

The symbolic circle can also become an imperfect shape, might appear as fragmented or fracturing, as this poem suggests:

My Mother is This White Wind Cleaning

out. Everything. From Grandma's house.
Laos is a refugee. Laos needs a place.
Laos is sponsored by her church—
those singing fundamentalists.

Out old clothes. Out thirty years of dirt.
Nothing's to be left.
Salvation's Army marches here—
converting love to modest rent.

Oh she has reasons heaped holy
on a silver platter, theological as
the head of John the Baptist.
Order, too. There's a box to Dump

there's a box for Goodwill, a box to Burn.
I'm reeling from them all.
I stay away and help. Late at night,
she asks me what I'll want to take.

"Save me Grandma's diaries, the morning
in June she called me outside to see
the salamander slide under the door,
odor of geraniums in the air.

Save me that place I slept and dreamed
for thirty years," I say.
She writhes. Gold rings twist themselves
around her fingers. She's down to blurt:

"All this must be done. Your aunt
and I are just sick of these decisions."
I nod. I know it is too late to teach
her to leave the soul of just one

earthly home alone or call it love's
unvendable estate. She knows not where
she comes from or where she goes.
She is borne again by her far God—

the cleansing homeless storm. I'm still
her son, the troublemaker. Here, growing,
a tree bent again by all her prevailing.
Where next, oh righteous tornado?

The illusion of superiority and centrality is probably necessary to the sustenance of culture. When rude encounters with reality shatter that illusion the culture itself is liable to decline.

Yi-Fu Tuan

The phone jangles. I leave the desk again. It is Elizabeth working late at the hospital in town. She tells me all the mountain passes—Cabbage Hill and Ladd Canyon—are closed. All the valley roads are a frozen impasse. No one can get in or out of the Grande Ronde tonight. Two hundred trucks have pulled off and parked. She wants to know if she should stay there and sleep at the hospital tonight. "Give me half an hour," I say, wondering how deep the drifts might be across our road by now, but not doubting my ability to get there and get her back here—somehow. That confidence is not built by chains and front-wheel drive alone. There is more to it. I hang up the phone and look around again: there is the larder on the porch full of peaches, applesauce, beans, mushrooms, pickles, chard, honey, peas, potatoes, Walla Walla sweets, lamb, trout, carrots—maybe five hundred pounds of food from the garden, pasture, mountains, rivers. Thinking of that abundance, I am stronger. The wood—split, stacked, dry lodgepole—four cords at least left: thinking of such work done, I am reassured. Putting on my wool hat, windbreaker, and boots, I remember Idaho winters under Mt. Spokane and how deep snow was a kind of joy for me. I check the fire, turn on the water, feel it cross my fingers cold, and go outside. The wind has died some. Looking back inside, I see the grandmother lamp burning—that single tongue of energy—but from outside, there are fewer reflections inward. The light seems more shallow—somehow. Above me, a white swirling mass breaks up as I head down the road to check the depth of the drifts, the shimmering white crust breaking like china plates under my boots. Behind me, I think of the beds, tools, diaries, children, cats, sheep, horses, sleds, stoves. Beside me, the dog—all mongrel confidence—trots along on top of the crust, the Puck of this mid-winter dream. Starving on Lolo summit, would I eat her?

～

If there's any discovery here, it may be that confidence is generated by marking the magic circle—the region—and asserting its centers. Even from biologists like Ardrey, we have learned that the animal who fights or defends home ground is doubly strong and likely to win. If not from biology, then from the mythic Antaeus we can see that defeat will come in battle only if he is abstracted into space. If not from myth, then from medicine we might be persuaded that the patient who heals at home heals faster and more surely than the patient who heals in hospital. If not from medicine, then from war, our war, Vietnam, we might learn that those who fought for home were impossible to kill, outnumber, even find. If not from war, then from the continuous assertions of small colleges and small town chambers of commerce who publicize that they are "the cultural, educational, and religious center of the intermountain west," or that they are "the regional center." This power of the magic circle to generate confidence also generates spiritual allies—strength, health, belief, optimism. Mere existence may go on elsewhere, but within the circle we thrive. The freight of weakness, helplessness, alienation, anguish—all that grinds without the bearings of the magic circle—is well known.

El Greco overcame those feelings by carrying clods of Cretan soil in his pockets all the time he lived in Spain. A northwest writer who moved to New York took a wall-sized photograph of Mt. Rainier with him for his office. If this confidence becomes excessive, it becomes dangerous; literally, chauvinism, less literally, nationalism. At its best, it is the result of love for home—that passion of Native Americans, 17th century Dutch, and others. This is never the same as love for a nation. Your region is not your nation. Thus, as the magic circle creates confidence, so the whole force of a region generates, nurtures, and sustains vitality, creativity, energy, delight.

Sometimes, that confidence comes from just one tree.

Larch in Fall

All my life I've seen you slowly going gold
slowly letting go your shade another year
felt your needles ticking down your limbs
to soothe the summer duff to sleep again—
your soft voice falling in October light.

Your gold tongue is spotfire on the ridge
saying silently that change must come where all
those changeless conifers believe that any turn
from official hue can mean the end, and still
you flare and freeze on steep north slopes.

In Idaho, you asked what color I would be.
I stared at you, said subtle green, said gold,
brown, black wet, and living in Montana
you gave me fence and roof and beams, and here
your form still gives me shape in cavities of snag.

You stand now as ghost women on the mountain whose
blood is sinking in my veins at night
whose double names I take to like confounding hope
whose heartwood is the tough straight muscle that
gives me light, whose fire is fire that speaks as

it burns up. I choose you, Larch, to all those
splattering loud leaves in hard and famous forests
in some country far from this interior, this west.
Hold to that ridge for me another year, hold to
that brilliance mottling the falling light
so still and clear—my changer who remains.

The circle and its four directions may be regarded as symbolic of the need for psychic orientation . . . In terms of psychological symbolism, the circle expresses the union of opposites—the union of the personal temporal world of the ego with the non-personal, timeless world of the non-ego.

Aniela Jaffe

The Toyota engine purrs steady on gas and oil from the Paleozoic swamps, the cylinders cast from Chinese ore. I wait, thinking of my wife at the hospital, wondering if when I met her hitchhiking in Spain she would ever have imagined herself, a sun-seeking Aussie, stranded on a December night in Oregon. (From nowhere comes the feeling that I'm suddenly writing this in a cave and looking out at Scotland.) The vehicle is warm now. Is the tenor? I shift to reverse. The frozen wheels break away from the red fir planks suddenly and I roll backward into the white road. As the lights swing over the fields, I recall the biggest drift at the highway and the night of the Pattersons' Christmas party thirteen years ago—before we moved out here from town. This same old blizzard suddenly began to blow while we were all inside drinking hot spiced wine. For us, the blizzard was new. No one had come prepared for 60 mph winds and freezing rain and snow. How could we have known? The ground was nearly bare. A few began to talk about leaving, but most stayed on. The wine was good, the Pattersons good hosts. I remember my friend Glen Davis—all confidence that his front-wheel drive could go through anything—plowed his Saab into that drift, high-centered, and he and his wife had to walk back up the hill to the party to save themselves. When they straggled in about midnight—Glen's beard frozen white and filled with ice, and Alice's whole body nearly frozen—some chose to leave their cars and ride in our old VW van which had better clearance, traction, and chains. We roared down the road past the high-centered Saab and luck got us to the highway where the Haufles, our future neighbors, were just being dropped off from a party. They began to attempt the 50 yard walk home through the drift against the driven snow and rain, the wife falling in the kneedeep freezing mass, the husband, bent by the wind, lifting her out. We waited in the van, watching them, and when she fell the second time and when we saw them hesitate and start back, two of us got out, went after them and brought them to the already-loaded van. There must have been fourteen of us packed like wet dogs in that old VW bus. Later, as Jean Haufle lay dying, she told me her red weasel dream, and asked me to give the eulogy at her funeral. I roll forward downhill, hitting drifts, blinded by snow, accelerating too high, slogging from side to side, the Toyota's front-wheel drive taking hold, the crust scraping the undercarriage as the bed of snow jostles me like a whale. I keep up the rpms like Joe Sander taught me and the big drift is there and I hit it and break through the berm of new-plowed snow onto the plowed highway feeling like I've suddenly been born. Fighting to slow down, sliding, turning into the slide, straightening out, on my way—I laugh.

Another value created by the magic circle is wholeness; appearing here in a brief winter road, so also found in the spiraling lines that reach out from the center of a region to the edges of time, place, memory, nature, sexuality. That growing from the center can go on forever, each experience laying on another growth ring over that first home—that place to stand. "Our life is an apprenticeship to the truth that around every circle another can be drawn; that there is no end in nature," says Emerson. That continuously enlarging circle, drawn and redrawn, but with its magic center sure, becomes a region's metaphor for the possibilities of wholeness. Turning inward, that circle can generate a life of continuous revelation—heartwood. Turned to nature, that circle can become ecological, asserting the unity of all life and requiring that we must come into harmonious relation with what we cannot create. In a region, in one watershed, in one household, that wholeness with nature is an individual possibility. I can oppose a dam on a local creek, a clearcut on a municipal watershed, a loss of local wilderness, and be effective. I cannot—fundamentally—generate the same demands for ecological wholeness elsewhere. Turned to human life, the circle invites a vision of human stability through resident generations, of human strength from families—their cycles, their picnics, their quarrels, their wisdom. From the long effects of time in place comes a kind of spiritual ecology, an intimate genealogy, a novel. Turned to individuals, the circle spirals away from mere acquaintances toward abiding friends.

Reports of those who only pass through the magic circle are likely to be tourist snapshots of a place still seeking mature portraiture. Yes, someone must be the wind, and the wind has its mystery, motion, depth, detail, and demands, but I'm willing to let someone else be the wind. I am studying how to know its local names—Chinook, Wallowa, Northwester—and how that wind feels when the barn door blows off on Columbus Day, how that wind shapes the trees, the people, the ridges, the prayers, and all of their relationships. Such a whole view creates a usable past, binds conscious to unconscious, dead to living, living to unborn, natural to human. Such unity is possible in a region, if it is possible at all. It takes years—sometimes—to just see something, as I was recently reminded:

From Half-Dead Grass

These infinite rise
all under town—purple, white—
quietly resurrecting dead lawns

with doubtless weeds.
Even before the cold trumpets
of hothouse Easter lilies

begin to preach gaudy white
in the crisscrossed churches
these small bright explosions

live and bloom through snow.
Why has it taken me
twelve years to see them

well enough to write this down:
Dwarf violets. Again.
In the cemetery. March 15.

〜

Through every human being, unique space, intimate space, opens up to the world.

Rilke

At the hospital, the parking lot is pure ice. I sit outside waiting for her, thinking of how far she is from the gumtrees, kookaburras, wallabies, kangaroos, koala bears, platypi, uncles, Merino sheep, aunts, brothers, horses, cousins, Murray Greys, drought, sunlight, beer, fruitcake—a whole other magic circle carried inside her. Eventually, she appears, full of stories, tired, coming home, coming down, my Scheherazade who saves our lives in stories: the 18-car wreck in the canyon, the scalp of Mrs. Awe from Spirit Lake, Idaho, sewn on and did I know her; three basins of blood and water to rinse out the glass fragments, the doctor changing his clothes three times; a baby born without pain; an old man setting himself on fire; a young man injured, drunk, and swearing; a nurse driving in through the storm who hasn't missed a nightshift in 20 years; her son, dying of cancer, stranded in Baker; who knows how long he has to live. We ride beyond the city's midnight, scrabble our way up the road home. Inside and warming by the fire, she tells me how many people are eating and sleeping overnight. Temporary shelters everywhere. We make tea and talk, her stories slowly letting us down from the blizzard's crisis. Undressing by the old lamp, her naked body softening in the light, her voice coming down to whisper as she pulls the quilts up over her ears, her hands on me freezing cold. We argue briefly about tomorrow's weather, I voting for the

15

returning sun, the solstice so near, and she voting for more cold—sure the world is against her. I find ways to warm her—old, familiar as lovers—and afterward she wants to trade sides of the bed. Mine must be warmer. I hear the stove cooling down ping by ping. Deer will come down again tonight to find the old Jonathans fallen under snow.

How does a region generate intimacy? In the magic circle, any experience can become a lover's dialogue—a shared story— because confidence allows anything to be said—right down to criticism that becomes encouragement, not simple correction. As I hear my wife's stories, so any dweller in the magic circle can be listening for that momentary revelation brought along by storm, calm, animal, plant, person, place. The exportable surface imagery of a region—the quaint postcard world of mountains, rivers, cowboys, loggers—tends to lose that intimacy imbedded in the fabric of daily lives. True intimacy can't travel outside the circle. Poets are always listening for those feelings and exploring them. All literature seeks—at its best—to further that intimate dialogue which nurtures and sustains the sacramental relation- ships on which our lives depend. Fed on public speeches from far away, we may all starve. Mass media can create mass malaise. Knowing the news doesn't mean anyone gives a damn.

Intimacy in a region also becomes the opening to universality. After I first learned the name of the rufous-sided towhee at Malheur Refuge, I gave myself to learning the names and lives of all those birds and now see more clearly when the tundra swans return from Argentina, when the robins return from Mexico. Once I was introduced by Ward Tonsfeldt to shaggy manes along the Clark Fork, I set out to find the real differences between toadstools and mushrooms, and followed those differences to the black woodear in the soups of China. Because I knew the story of the Chinese miners murdered on the Snake River, I lived cau- tiously in Hunan Province for a year, though I did see the *guo gi* (wild chicken) in the marketplace—the bird whose cry surrounds the edges of northwest grainfields, whose flashing neck and feathered rainbow explodes out of dry grass by the river. Going to The College of Idaho with Tom Jaramillo, Raul Welder, Jose Nasser, it was easier to live undergraduate years in Ecuador and Spain and understand that Spanish is not just a foreign language—it marks another magic circle which can be revealed to anyone who refuses to become a tourist. Thus, the intimate within the region becomes the opening to the universal—the needle's eye holds the binding thread of everywhere. The ancient fight for that intimacy goes on and on:

Voice from Another Wilderness

A long time
we were living old
in the north before the Romans.

We watched them march.
They wanted slaves.
Our fists tightened on our spears.

We strung our bows
with fierce belief
and waited for the dark. Romans are easy

to kill at night.
They cannot see us
painted as we are with clay and ash.

We fight them now
for everything we love—
our deer, our wives, our trees.

They say Romans will never
go home. We can't leave these hills.
Tonight, we attack the garrison and retreat.

Be with us, gods
of the river. Caves
in the mountains, wait for us.

Caractacus, we come.

*From the shapes of men's lives imparted by the places where they
have experience, good writing comes.*

William Carlos Williams

Here, it is morning now. Long dreaming drifts have laid their
curves high and deep across the roads. Public power is still off.
Not even the mailman or the paper carrier will make it through
today. White shifting skiffs of snow still move over the fields
flowing like currents over riverbed. I build up the fire again and
the stovepipe begins to ping, the drafts wheeze, the fly ash circles
softly upward, then disappears. Water for coffee heats on the
stove. But for the skittish wind, there is no movement outside. I
wait at the desk. Suddenly, a red-shafted flicker lights among the
ice-glazed branches of the apple tree and begins to peck its way
into a frozen core. I watch that black half-moon on its breast as it
pecks, stops, a black shining eye cast upward, then pecks again.
In the frozen field, the horses wait for their oats and alfalfa and I
see the shapes of two pheasants by their feeders—*guo gi* picking
up the smallest kernels of grain. Everyone still sleeps. I close the
draft and damper on the stove. The dog has finished her morning
dance and whine and is ready to go out. At the open door, I see
the Blue Mountains darkened with pine, the lower slopes open,
white, smooth. I remember my earliest crayon-scribbled pictures

on that heavy paper from grade school: huge white mountains in the background, low green hills, creek coming down blue with black stones, a gabled house in the center, smoke scrawling gray out the chimney, a few people with hats. I think of my grandfathers and grandmothers in their coastal graves in the shadows of Rainier, of my wife and children in their inland beds asleep, of the Columbia waiting for all our lives to melt as this snow will soon. I go inside to the silence, surrounded by the old wood walls with openings to the light, openings leaking wind. It is warm. I will make Elizabeth some coffee now.

A region is a microcosm—a magic circle centered on *home.* The values generated by that circle are many, but I have limited myself here to three—confidence, wholeness, and intimacy. For me, the authentic map of the universe is composed of these microcosms—domes of specific human light, crossing all abstract political, geographic, economic, and racial boundaries. This view of region as *microcosm* stands in contrast to the more dangerous notion of region as *province.* When defined as *province,* region becomes an edge in a far remote place, a fragment of some empire with a far-away center. When the magic circle is defined as *province,* local life can be drained of significance, since only those who live at the center are real. Thus, local intimacy, confidence, and wholeness are threatened. In contrast, region as *microcosm* enables an artist living anywhere—including the Northwest—to get work done, to achieve character, belief, aesthetic, purpose, and style. Region as *province* imposes a centralizing political and demographic metaphor which can artificially elevate the significance of artists who live in political or population centers, and artificially dismiss significant artistic achievements that are not centralized by nonartistic forces. An artist who chooses not to live in political or population centers, who chooses not to become an alien to the oldest and most immediate sources of human nurture, who chooses not to become a victim of nationalism—such an artist must assert the region as *microcosm*—this locust flowering, that hive by the Columbia—and where do you live?

Venn Confesses an Early Crime

One Sunday afternoon when I was nine
my family all asleep in the holy cold silence
of our Presbyterian manse in Burlington,
I snuck out alone to see the April afternoon.
Dandelions bloomed on the church lawns
like Straight Arrow's golden rings.
No one was around, not even a lost dog.
I remembered my hunger and the empties
behind the store on Fairhaven Avenue.

I went there and pulled three pop bottles
through the slats and toted them around
to the front, thinking of Sugar Ray Robinson
in the bubblegum pack, or maybe I was wanting
a Big Hunk or a Mountain Bar or Royal Crown—
a boy gets hungry on Sunday afternoon alone.
I raised my matchless bottles to the counter
and waited for my pennies, but the owner said
he saw me stealing and gripped me like God

until my stepfather, His solid minister, came
with His hard stick and spanked me two blocks
home. He is dying now as I remember that day
and still empties nod to me everywhere I go.
They comfort me somehow the way they wait, so
carelessly cast away, such luck. In the waste
of big people, Sunday School, and Jesus Loves Me
a boy needed something definite to find and do.
That was my life then—small stealing, rescuing

rejection.

The First Day of Summer

Swaying in the evergreen crown, he tightened his grip around the green limbs. Clear pitch stuck to his fingers from the breaking bark—silver-gray, smooth, close. The odor of turpentine. Hanging on there at the top of the fir as though he were a flag of blue jeans and gray sweatshirt, he did not answer his grandmother's calling. He could see her through the branches—a small, white-haired figure far to the south. The wind lifted his brown hair, made his eyes water, swayed him. He shifted his grip, moved his rubber boots tight against the thin trunk where he knew the branches would not break, then looked up as the pair of old crows circled above him—cawing, making dives, cawing, flying away, coming back. Eastward, he saw the pasture and white sheep. The lambs looked like rabbits as they chased each other through the green bracken. Above the sheep, the green-timbered hills, the cold white mountain, a cap of cloud. His cousins lived in that direction. One crow dove at him and he ducked his head under his arm as the wild caw went over. He looked down through the green mass of limbs and needles to the crow's nest full of black feathers and pink throats squawking, flopping, collapsing. One fledgling flew out, fell, flew, caught itself in another tree. Maybe he could catch that one, feed it bread and milk, cut its tongue, teach it to talk.

His grandmother had stopped calling him now and he watched as she turned and left the back porch of the farmhouse. A mile to the north, he could see another red farmhouse across the swamp. Smoke rising in a blue swirl against the timbered hills. Solid second-growth green. Alice lived there. He flexed his hands that gripped the green limbs and felt the evergreen sway again. An ache began to build in the arches of his feet. The pitch between his fingers was like glue. He saw it was already turning black on his palms. Keeping his boots close to the trunk, moving carefully and slowly, he began to descend the eighty feet to the ground. He always came here for summers. He felt he belonged here—this small farm on the way to the mountain. Going down branch by branch, he stopped to watch the fledgling crows in their nest. They were silent now. An old crow glided through the limbs above him. He knew that underneath those birds would be bones, safety pins, tinsel, spoons, bottlecaps—anything shining. He had seen such nests before. He continued down, remembering his uncle's pond to the west where he would swim with his cousins— eye to eye with bullfrogs—on the hot days in August. Here, he didn't have to be the preacher's adopted son, the one whose father died. Here, he could be George and Hazel Leland's grandson. Here, Tacoma and his last day in the 8th grade—yesterday—could be forgotten.

Dropping from the last limb to the ground, he looked up again toward the black tangle of the crow's nest. He put his hands on the fir trunk and walked slowly around it, always looking up through the limbs. The old crows were silent now. He could see the one fledgling perched alone. Tomorrow, he would come back for it. Tomorrow. Around him, silence and the green shamrock blooming white and delicate against the thick duff of castoff needles and cones, silence and thick brown trunks of evergreens, silence and one pitch seam running amber, streaking white, silence and the clear June light gold and deep around him.

He left the fir grove like a bear cub—rolling through the blackberries, salmonberries, swordfern and maidenhair, bracken and swampgrass. He crawled on his hands and knees into old burned stump piles, he walked a cedar windfall across a skunk-cabbage swamp, he watched the ants eating their way through a gigantic red rotting log, he counted the red berries on a devil's club. He moved easily, silently, carefully. Burrs caught in his cuffs, thorns held his sleeves, webs crossed his face. Still, he moved easily.

When he came to the creek, he lay down on his belly, sure nobody could find him there. He watched the shimmering water move, listened to its gurgle against the bank of buttercups. The water skippers went sliding out over the eddy, their shadows crossing the bottom as small dots; the tufts of green moss clung to the rocks; the periwinkles held on just under the surface like mosaics of small stones. He put his hands into the creek and lifted the clear cold water to his mouth, then saw the black pitch staining his hands, so he leaned over the bank and drank like a deer, sucking the water up into him, holding his breath and swallowing. As the cold water filled him, his teeth began to ache and he heaved himself up, away, back—all in a single move—and let out his breath with a burst of spray. He thought of his dead father's saxophone in the attic where he had slept last night. It was in the black case, but when he opened it one day last summer, the instrument gleamed at him—like something in a dream—and he had taken it out of the blue soft padding and tried to play its cold silver body without a reed. The sound had terrified him and he put the instrument away quickly.

He left the creek for red thimbleberries and ate a handful of the soft buttons of fruit, then climbed a vine maple crotch by crotch until he could climb no higher. At the top, he swung out into the air and felt the branch give and his heart pound as the branch slowly bent to the ground without breaking. "Alle alle autsun free," he said aloud. When he touched the ground, he held onto the branch a moment, staring at the green tight thin bark, then let the vine maple snap back upright—sudden and green. When his brother came in a few weeks, they would play here for hours. The game was to swing from clump to clump without touching the ground. The game was to pretend to be Tarzan. The game was to find the best crotch for a slingshot and mark the place to come back to. His last slingshot had been confiscated by his stepfather, the preacher, in Tacoma. He'd broken a window in the huge brown church by accident.

He went on then, looking in hollow logs for skunks and rabbits, stirring up the red ant hill, throwing rocks at the yellowjackets' nest. Seeing the red and orange salmonberries ripening around him, he reached out for them, tasted them sour and seed-filled and sometimes sweet. He did not mind. He remembered August, the wild blackberries ripening. They were best behind the barn on the old rotten logs. He stopped to watch a mole heaving up a new mound suddenly before him.

He hid behind the fire-blackened cedar snag, its top like a fractured bone. He had seen the red-headed woodpecker drumming there in the morning early. Now, peering out from behind a charcoal root, he saw his grandparents going into the barn. On his belly, he crawled elbows and knees through the grass and ferns and put his eye to a crack in the boards. The odor of sheep and goats. He heard his grandmother talking, but could not see her.

"It's Ruth. Over there in the corner." Hazel Leland watched as her husband slowly walked with his two metal canes to the one sheep still in the barn, the last pregnant ewe. It was well past noon. "What's wrong?" Karl could see his grandfather wince as he bent to feel the ewe. His knees had gotten worse since retirement.

"I thought she might be cast or in labor, but she don't want to get up," George Leland said.

"What should we do?"

"Probably be dead by tonight."

"Well, with Karl here, we could use the meat."

"No. She might have the fever. You can't tell."

"Where's Karl, anyway? He didn't come up for lunch."

"Down in the woods, I guess."

"Well, I been waiting all month to have the lawn mowed."

He pulled back from the barn like an Indian spy, like he had come upon danger and had to escape it. He crawled back into the tall cool ferns, down the bank to the creek, crossed in a leap, slipped into the trees again, and in the trees he walked into the pure density of vegetation where camouflage was sure. He came, in an hour, to an old-growth cedar stump left by his old cousins from Germany in 1895. Out of the second-growth alder, the old silver stump rose like a monument. From the impossible density where its fluted roots began, the stump curved upward ten feet to a circular top flattened by old crosscutting saws. Karl had found and made many camps in these woods, but this was his most important one. With his hands, he traced the step he had chopped into the cedar's largest root the first year he'd found this stump. He raised one boot into that first step and, balancing himself, lifted the other boot to the springboard notch, then pulled his first boot up into the notch too. His cousins had once stood here to fall the tree. Resting there, he then reached out to the huckleberry bush on the top and pulled himself upward, his boots scraping and slipping wildly. On top, the empty center opened. He smiled. A beam of light touched his ring of blackened stones and crossed the rungs of a crude ladder he'd made of saplings last summer. In one of the roots, he saw the wooden powder box stashed. Pitch sticks, matches, smoked smelt, comic books, salt, candles, fishing line, hooks, and kerosene lantern—all his stuff—would be waiting. The brown bracken covering the dirt floor of the stump would need to be replaced with fresh green fronds. He could do that today. Looking around, he climbed down into the hollow center, satisfied that no one had followed him, that he was alone.

Looking up, he could only see the circle the stump made— green leaves and gray branches filled with shifting shapes of blue sky and white cloud, and one still huckleberry bush spreading its rounding leaves, the green navels of new huckleberries growing beneath them. Quiet. He put his hand against the old cedar, felt it strong, dry, solid beneath his touch. Quiet.

He remembered how the collie had come here that summer night, how she had crawled under the roots, through a hole he had never seen, how her cold nose had awakened him, how he had listened as she had borne her puppies back in one of the deepest roots, how she had kept them there and let him put a gunnysack under them.

He climbed the ladder and sat there on the moss-covered cedar rim beside the huckleberrry bush. Green wilderness spread around him. One bird flitted through the undergrowth below—a brown wren. All around him rose thick columns of silver-gray alder trees tapering into a dense green canopy swaying over him in the June wind. He was not hungry. He wanted to be still, to see. He would wait for something to move. A deer. A grouse. Alice. "Alle alle autsun free," he said softly. "Alle alle autsun free."

"Ah, there you are, Karl. I was wondering." His grandfather stopped splitting kindling in the woodshed. Karl watched the round, strong, kind face, the jaw muscles, the streaks of white hair below the brown cap. His grandfather made him think of a bear. His shoulders were heavy, rounded, thick. His forearms and hands holding the shining ax were the largest Karl had ever seen.

"What you doing, Grandpa?" Karl asked. He'd been watching him through the slats of the shed for some time. It was getting dark now and it felt like rain. George Leland turned to his grandson.

"Take these chunks and that diesel out in the pasture, will you, boy?"

"What you gonna do, Gramp?" Karl said.

"We gotta burn that dead ewe in the barn."

"What for?"

"Confound it, boy. Just do what I tell you." Karl looked at his grandfather, then looked away. He picked up the armload of split cedar and the can of diesel and went out into the pasture where he saw a pile of cedar posts—the ends rotted off. His grandfather came slowly after him, a cane in each hand. His red-black plaid jacket flapped in the wind.

"Now, get the ewe, Karl. Think you can do it?"

"But she's still alive, Grandpa. I saw her."

"Well, she oughta be dead. Just go get her now."

When Karl walked down to the barn again, the ewe bleated at him, one green eye glistening in the dim light through the cob-webbed windows. He hesitated, trying to think of ways to save her. He offered her oats from his pitchy hand, but she would not open her mouth. He tried to lift her to her feet, but she would not roll up. He went around behind her and pinched her hard at the base of her tail, but she still just lay there on her side. The odor of sheep, manure, urine-soaked bedding. He knew his grandfather wouldn't change his mind with that tone of voice. It didn't sound like his grandfather, but reminded him of his stepfather's voice back in Tacoma, and some Sunday School teachers who always got angry when he asked them why he was *lost* and *going to hell* and why everything was *God's will.* Just do it. Do what I say. You'll never understand it. He heard his grandfather now calling his name, so he grabbed the ewe by the hind legs and dragged her out from under the stairs, across the manure and straw of winter, and out to his grandfather waiting in the pasture dusk. The ewe was stiff, heavy, bloated, full of lambs. She bleated now and then and tried to hold her head up to see where she was going. Karl could feel a fine mist beginning to fall on his face. It silvered his grandfather's jacket and made the pasture seem to shine.

"Better go get the shotgun, Karl," his grandfather said.

"What should I tell Grandma?"

"Just say I want it, and hurry."

In the house he had successfully avoided all day, he went quietly to his grandfather's bedroom, lifted the 12-gauge shotgun off the rack, and started outside. Hazel Leland had heard him and met him on the porch.

"Where do you think you're going with that? And where have you been?"

"Gramp wants it." He held the shotgun out to her.

"Get that thing away from me."

"Can I go?"

"Did he tell you to?"

"Yes."

"Well, hurry up. Dinner's almost ready."

Hazel Leland walked to the porch corner past the bag of chicken scratch, turned on the yard light and watched as Karl went out into the pasture. After the boy had handed the shotgun to his grandfather, Hazel shouted clearly and authoritatively: "Father, send Karl in now."

"Should I go, Gramp?" Karl asked.

"Stay here. You're old enough to help."

"Gramp says I should help him," Karl shouted to his grandmother.

"All right for you, Father. It's on your soul, not mine."

She slammed the back door, rattling the glass, then stood inside watching them work in the pasture. She could see the rest of their flock of sheep coming toward the barn now—Mary and Martha and Eve and Lot's Wife, the ewes, and Cain and Abel, the wethers, and Abraham, the ram, and the lambs without names running among them playing. She did not approve of boys helping with such work. It could give them bad dreams. After butchering, she had seen children who'd watched wake screaming.

"Where's the shell?"

"Here, Gramp. I brought two."

"Only need one, boy. You figger I'd miss?"

"I don't know, Grandpa," Karl said. He was afraid now, but did not know why. He felt like he wanted to run, to hide, to not come out again. He looked for his grandfather's face, but could not see it. The night mist still fell around them, separating them.

"You want to kill her or should I?" his grandfather said.

"I don't know where to aim and all that—"

"Look the other way," George Leland said.

Karl stepped back, tripped over the ewe, and fell on his back in the wet grass. He saw the dark form of his grandfather moving toward the ewe. He heard the metallic slip and lock of the shotgun's action, the slow swishing of his grandfather's boots. He had to heave himself over, scramble on his hands and knees. The old man was unsteady without his canes. He was coming to shoot. When he was far enough away, Karl stopped, turned, and saw his grandfather lifting the gun to his shoulder and holding the muzzle behind the ewe's drooping ear.

"Look the other way now, Karl," his grandfather said, then the gun flashed in the dark and the skull shattered and a piece hit Karl's boot and lay shining in front of him like an oyster shell. He heard his grandfather mumble, heard him eject the empty shell. Karl wondered about the lambs inside, about the ticks on her body. "Let's get her on the fire, boy." Karl felt his stomach begin to heave. Choking back the sour in his throat and nose, spitting it on the grass, Karl took the dead ewe by the front legs and his grandfather took her by the back legs. Together, they dragged her, the bloody head slogging from side to side. Karl tried to obey his grandfather and get her pulled up over the post pile, but she was heavy, awkward, unwieldy. She flopped away from him and Kark fell into the wood. He rolled and he fell under her. The wet grass was like ice to him. It seemed like hours before they had her in place—draped across the wood, her belly down. Then he watched as his grandfather drenched the ewe and the wood with diesel and lit the kindling. It flickered small and deep under the pile where paper and dry wood fed the flames, then gradually the fire began to flare upward until the darkened pasture, glazed now with light rain, began to glisten and reflect back the light of the fire. The other sheep came forward now, staring, standing, the fire reflecting red off their eyes. Karl watched them—motionless humps of wool glowing in the dark. A lamb bleated—lost from its ewe. Why would they come to see this, Karl wondered. He turned back to the fire and saw the wool had begun to singe black in the flames but not burn. He began to think the ewe wasn't dead, that the lambs inside her were alive, that what he saw was not a sheep. It was something else, something terrible, someone he didn't know. He looked away.

"You don't like this much, do you, boy?"

"Do you?"

"Somebody's got to do it. We gotta look out for the rest of them or first thing you know, they might all be dead."

"What about the—the lambs?" Karl said.

"You'd have to be a vet."

"There must be something—"

"No way around it, boy, no way around it at all. Now throw a little more diesel on her, Karl. We don't want any of those worms getting out alive."

Karl stood motionless, staring at the fire, at the ewe's body stretched across it. Looking up, he could see his grandmother standing inside the back porch. He felt suddenly heavy, sick to his stomach again. He wished she would call him now. His grandfather sat back down on a shakebolt, the shotgun still in his hand.

"Well, are you helping me or aren't you?"

"I don't feel good."

"Little green around the gills, eh? Better go on in, Karl."

Karl backed away from the bonfire, and when he felt as though his grandfather could no longer see him, he turned and ran toward the house. His grandmother opened the back door.

"When's Father coming in?"

"I don't know. He said I could go."

"Why'd you run off all day?"

"I was just down in the woods," he said.

"Phew! You stink!"

"Where?"

"Just look at you. Just filthy dirty. And look at those hands."

By the light from the kitchen, Karl could see his hands stained red with the ewe's blood. He had not known.

"It's just a little blood, Grandma," he said.

"Why didn't you come when I called you for lunch?"

"I didn't hear you," he lied.

"Well, get your boots off. Dinner's about ready."

"I'm not very hungry," he said.

"It's your favorite: lemon pie. I made it for you."

"Oh, I ate a lot of berries."

"Well, berries won't fill you up. A boy needs three good meals a day. Now get those boots off. You've got to get cleaned up." When his grandmother finished, she opened the door and shouted, "Dinnertime" to George Leland, who still sat watching the fire. "I think he likes it," she said. "It's the only thing he's done all day."

Karl sat alone on the back porch. He felt sick. He wanted to run, he wanted to sleep. The glare of the bonfire shifted up and down on the walls around him now. In the kitchen, he could see his grandmother at the breadboard rolling out biscuits, her hands covered with flour. Slowly, he pulled off his rubber boots, then went in. The sweet smell of chicken frying. He felt like there was a lump in his belly that would not dissolve. He felt suddenly tired. His face began to warm. Kettles of vegetables were steaming on the stove. He saw the two round lemon pies with the browned tips of meringue on the counter. The table was set for three of them. He looked at his hands. They were red with blood. He was afraid. He hid them from his grandmother and filled the sink with water. He washed with lava soap until his knuckles were red. The pitch would not come off. He felt his face flush now. It was hot in the kitchen. His stomach roiled.

"Here. Get to it," his grandmother said. She handed him a green coffee can two-thirds full of white grease flecked with brown bits of meat. He dipped in his finger, took a lump of grease, and began to wrap his hands around and around each other to get off the pitch, each finger shining as the grease dissolved the signs of play on limbs he had held to earlier that day. "Now don't get that on the floor. I just waxed this afternoon. You better do that over the sink." When she turned to slide the biscuits in the oven, he snitched a bit of raw biscuit dough. "And wipe off on that paper towel," she said. She lifted a strand of gray hair behind her ear, a strand that had come loose from her bun tightly braided and pinned to the back of her head. When his grandfather came in, he washed his hands at the sink and they all sat down.

They held hands, as they always did, and they bowed their heads and closed their eyes, except Karl, who watched as his grandmother said the blessing: "Our Father, we thank Thee for this food, bless it to our use and us in Thy service. We thank Thee for bringing Karl safely to us for another summer. Go with us and guide us. In Jesus' name, Amen." Karl pretended to be opening his eyes and looked up and sighed inaudibly as his grandparents always did. He took small portions of the overcooked peas and carrots, boiled potatoes and gravy, and fried chicken. They teased him about eating like a girl and reminded him that he had two hollow legs last summer, so he had a second helping of everything. His grandmother got up to serve the lemon pie, then came back and stared at Karl's head.

"What's that in your hair?"

"I don't know. Where?"

"Right there." She pointed and touched a wad in his hair. "Oh, it's pitch." She sounded disgusted.

"Pitch," he said.

"You've got pitch in your hair. We'll get it out after dinner."

His grandfather ate ravenously throughout the meal and after dinner he excused himself and said he was going out to tend the fire.

"Can I go outside for a while?" Karl asked.

"You better stay in now. It's late," his grandmother said. She had gone to rummage in a drawer for a pair of scissors—old ones.

"But Gramp might need some help."

"Let's get you taken care of," she said.

He turned and saw her coming toward him with the sharp scissors in her hand. She had greased them, and carried a piece of paper towel over her arm. "Sit down here." He sat down. Out the window, the fire looked like a monster with one orange eye. As his grandfather worked, sudden explosions of sparks and flaming brands flew upward in the night and went out. He felt his grandmother brushing his hair away and heard the scissors begin to snip. He felt their cold steel against his scalp and shivered.

"Sit still now, I'm just about done."

"O.K.," he said.

"How on earth did you get pitch in your hair?"

"Climbing trees," he said.

"Is that what you did all day?"

"Just played."

"You better stick around tomorrow. There's lots of work to be done," she said and thrust in front of him a swatch of his thick brown hair matted with pitch. He wanted to run. He knew she would never follow him into the woods. His grandfather would stop at the fence. They might shine flashlights after him, but their voices would be too weak to call him back. He stared at his hair. A sudden helplessness washed over him. He watched his grandmother throw the pitch and hair into the cookstove.

"Can I go to bed now?" he said.

"You better take a bath first," she said.

"I'm too tired."

"Well, brush your teeth. Your bed is made up with fresh quilts." He felt the bare spot on his head where she'd cut away the pitch from him. It was cold there now.

"Goodnight, Grandma," he said and kissed her, then went upstairs. The sound of light rain on the cedar shakes. The roof lulled him to sleep.

A Gallon of Honey
in Glass

Here—a sweet stone
to ride your shelf
a lost summer
given shape to last.

Here—what keeps
guarded by stinging.
This is your voice
whispering "Home."

Here, the perfect
field is flowing
against the bitter
that winter brings.

The specks of wax
will hope to feel
your slowly stare.
Savor such light

as your tongue can say.
Thousands and thousands
of shimmering things
have brought you love.

Here is proof.
Dip in your hands.

Part II

The Trail to School

This landowner thinks he's rich
but weeds lord all his ground.
They carry me—cheat and foxtail—
over his broken stile.

In a fallow field, I hear
the property belongs to banks.
The tenant farmer's dog comes out
then stalks my tracks.

This pasture's owned by Widow Jean
whose perfect yard I mark.
Her grass I call a Mushroom Town.
For mayor, I nominate the moon.

Across the road, I walk the freehold
of the Church. They built
this fort for God's Indian trade.
The factor calls me Skulk.

Over another fence, I'm on open land
owned by creeks and meadowlarks,
hawks and wind. Each sound is a deed.
Their courthouse is my ear.

Vaulting the chain link fence,
I fall into the library of death.
The grass is mowed. Plastics flinch
by the stone books holding breath

as I pass. Now seventh is the state.
The field's open, flat, and green.
Harvest here is balls and bats
and children's screams.

I steal my shadow over this trail.
Trespass is my name.
I am the black wolf of love.
Nothing is mine. I just go around.

A Note for Primary Art

In the alley behind our house at dusk, I stood next to a shining juice can watching for my friends. They had to be hidden close by, waiting for the chance to sprint and kick that juice can to kingdom come. If I saw them first, I yelled, "Over the can on David," and if I jumped over the can at the same time, David was *out*. Over the darkening neighborhood, anyone could hear us—those noisy grade school kids—playing kick-the-can. Now, I saw Frank Younger chugging from the garage to the walnut tree. I yelled, "Over the can on Frankie Exemblub," and he came out from behind the tree and stood with me. "Last one caught is *it*," he puffed, and waited by the can while I made a few forays down the alley and back so as not to be called a "base sticker." (Earlier, of course, we'd gone through *eenie, meenie, miney, mo* to decide who was *it*.) I was just about to catch Dave Wollen behind the garbage can when my mother called me to supper. I asked Frankie if he wanted to be *it*. He said no. He had to go. I looked around once more, then yelled out: "Alle alle autsun free, alle alle autsun free." I still don't know where I learned the phrase, but it told everyone hiding that our game was over. Like sandman shadows, they all came in. Somebody stood on top of the can, then somebody else kicked it out from under him and kicked it rattling down the street. We all went in for dinner. Our play seemed to be always like this: made possible by a few words that we all knew and liked to say at critical moments—beginning, choosing, criticizing, ending.

Even before first grade, this daily poetry played around our ears in ways that delighted us. How old were we when, toweling off after a bath, we learned to name the five famous beasts: To Market, Stayed Home, Roast Beef, None, and Wee Wee Wee All-The-Way-Home? Such names and their rhythms became part of our toes, our toes turned to piglets, piglets to little sausages the next morning. There was no resisting the laughter on the little toe when somebody changed the rhyme to Pee Pee Pee All-The-Way-Home. We didn't know, of course, that these were almost perfect parallels worked to climax with narrative. In the same fashion, we didn't know anything about syllabics when Grandpa said to sit on his lap and close your eyes and see if you can keep from laughing while I say this:

Knock on the door (*tap the forehead*)
Peek in (*lift an eyelid*)
Lift up the latch (*raise the chin*)
Walk in (*tickling the throat and chest*)

We heard the anticipation in each line, the tension enlarging, and learned that this was play, the eye was a window, the mind a door, and fingers feet, and more and do it again. Even sitting on Grandma's knee going up and down in rhythm to *Horsie goes walking, walking; horsie goes trit-trot, trit-trot; horsie goes cantering, cantering; horsie goes galloping, galloping,* we had no way of knowing that this was sound play also. Again, that play was made with more than Grandma's feet.

To this wealth of games and rhymes from home, school added other kinds of primary verbal play, but most of that wasn't learned in the classroom. In jumprope, we heard the surprise in *Cinderella, dressed in yella/went upstairs to kiss a fella/made a mistake and kissed a snake.* In the hallways, we learned the most basic indirections—*your barn door's open* and *XYZ* (examine your zipper). In simple playground liar liar chants, in the *I-slit-a-sheet* tongue twisters, in the parodies of hickory dickory, in the arribarribooski nonsense, in stumpranchingtripeeatingleatherheadedtuboflard curses, in traveling salesman knock knock elephant Polack jokes, in handclap rhymes—all of these began to take us by the ears, showing us the possible shapes for sound that would coerce our attention, for sound that wouldn't leave us as indifferent as the talk talk talk of the teacher in the classroom.

All of these traditional sources of playing around with words confirmed for us, before we even knew it, that words were a primary means to delight, discovery, risk, love, community, power, and play. Given enough jangle and freedom, this sense of language generated by traditional folk art can become a means to define, enrich, and sustain poetry. For instance, when Alistair Reid begins: "Curiosity may have killed the cat;/ more likely the cat was just unlucky . . .", that poet has used a traditional saying as an entrance to his poem. When Dylan Thomas wrote "Once *below* a time" in "Fern Hill," he knew the traditional folk style and chose to ask it, there, to create surprise. When Theodore Roethke came to define what he liked in poetry, he first quoted this traditional rhyme:

Hinx, minx, the old witch winks,
the fat begins to fry;
nobody home but Jumping Joan,
Father, Mother, and I.

When James Joyce came to the writing of *Finnegan's Wake*, which may be verbal play at its contemporary extreme, he makes reference to more than seventy of what are sometimes too easily called "nursery rhymes," using them to embody the recurring motifs of human experience. When Arthur Miller wrote *Death of a Salesman*, much of the basic imagery had, in a sense, been prepared for him by the countless traveling salesman jokes which had circulated among us for years. These, of course, are simply a few instances in which what is sometimes called *art* derives definition, enrichment, and sustenance from a more primary tradition.

Removed from the delight, risk, love, community, and play that folk tradition embodies, there are a multitude of consequences. The most obvious is the reduction of poetry from verbal play to poetry as disguised sermonette, a habit which seems to be perfected in public education. Another consequence, more related to poet than audience, is the loss of primary imagery such as the "red herring" in this traditional poem:

A man in the wilderness asked me,
How many strawberries grow in the sea.
I answered him, as I thought good,
As many red herrings as swim in the wood.

A final consequence of being removed from the qualities of folk tradition I find embodied in some lines from William Carlos Williams's poem "To Elsie." Opening with the line, "The pure products of America/ go crazy—," Williams develops a catalog of the damned, then identifies their fate:

to be tricked out . . .
with gauds
from imaginations which have no

peasant traditions to give them
character
but flutter and flaunt

sheer rags—succumbing without
emotion
save numbed terror . . .

In the face of much that is called modern, I sense that perhaps we need to remind ourselves that gauds, terror, and rags don't preserve, enrich, or sustain all that is human. Even in *alle alle autsun free, over the can on Frankie Exemblub,* and *eenie, meenie, miney, mo,* we still have sources for the nurture of our lives and our poetry. At least, if we recognize the wealth of traditional folk poetry, even in balladry, we might be able to hold on to verbal play in our critical moments. We might even remember to answer nonsense with nonsense. Most of all, we won't have to work and worry ourselves to death by believing that primary delight in words must be outgrown after the sixth grade is over.

~

Poem Against the First Grade

for Alicia and Alex

Alex, my son, with backberry jam
smeared ear to ear and laughing,
rides his unbroken joy with words
so fast we let him get away
on the jamjar without clean cheeks first.

He spills frasasass
tea with milk and honey;
a red-chafted schlicker
beats our cottonwood drum.
Thumping the pano keys
like a mudpie chef,
he goes wild with words
at the wittle wooden
arms inside, a hundred
Pinoschios to singsong.
If he can't wide byebye
bike to the candy store,
where he is Master Rich
with one penny, words turn
to tears in his mouf. Once
in a while, he walks home
with pumpumpumpernickel bread,
his nose twitching so fast
a wabbit would love him.

Now this language isn't taught in first grade.
Alicia, his tister, knows this *fact*.
But he juggles it around all day
until she makes him spit it out like
a catseye marble or a tack. "Ax," she says,
"that's not *right*." She's been among giants
who wipe off the dialect of backberry jam,
then pour hot wax on each bright mistake.

I hope for a bad seal on Ax and tister,
encourage the mold of joyous error
that proper sad giants, armed to the ears
with pencils and rules, all forgot.

❧

The Office

Every morning, I open these
two windows looking west
let out the living flies
blow their dead away
let the wind in again
when it knocks at the big panes.
Through these old openings
studious yellowjackets visit me.
What they want they always say:
"We're here to teach you how
to write. Watch now: we're flying
the first word you need to scrawl."

Soon, students hammer at the door
poke their tentative heads inside.
I ask them what they want of me
and most of them aren't sure—
some kind of map for their wandering
toward names. Among them I've found
slugs, wolves, dreamers, bores.
A few I don't have to fight to love.
A few want to carry me away, a few
come back year after year to say—
Their blizzard of paper sifts under
my door day into day, drifts over
the dictionary, covers my head gone gray.
I bite my pencil and go on with praise.

Don't try to fool me, room.
Your walls are built of bread
but my life is not here with
these phones and memoranda
with these steel files with drawers
like morgues. No, room, my life
is outside riding blue bicycles—
no hands—down the dark morning
streets delivering poems real as
Sunday papers to every porch
with a slam, hoping for that sudden
awakening, those lights going on
within and within.

Now, this is the news
for the writing class next door:
I am not a salt block or a hurdle
or your father or your grader.
I do not teach for money, power,
or any degrees of empty publicity.
I bring you only what yellowjackets
have taught me—a kind of song
you must learn to listen for
that comes from opening your windows
and closing your door every day for years.
Can you hear it now?

Fourteen Modes of Local Discourse
in the Composing Process

Are you the one who will
revise me again? Is this pure
sensuous attention?
Will you turn me to salt
on a stick, then wander out?
What? I may not call you that.
Ask me. "Yes" is always the answer.

***

Mushrooming the canyon? No.
I'd have left you there.
You picked my class because
it fit your emptiness and now
you're here spawning your soul
in single-spaced faint pica.
Tell me, how can you audit this?

***

"When things are tough, I improvise,"
he wrote, and told me once about
those drift fences he stood up in spring
after the snow had gone from the mountains
and how he laid them all down in fall.
Where are you now, cowboy? Bucking bales?

***

Pour a jug of cold wind
on your tears. They'll dry.
The hell you cause the world
becomes your only cry.
The new question now is grow.
Yes, you need this class
but go plant radishes first
take a long walk by the river.
Let go.

* * *

Remember that day you risked
every limb to get your apples down
while I held on below
catching what you dropped
hoping my grip was good enough
to hold you up
in that unsteady air?

* * *

After class, you are still here
with the empty cans, waiting
with the abandoned books. Yes,
come in. No, I don't have anything
to do. It's 5:30, Friday afternoon.
Yes, start with your childhood again.

* * *

Look out the window now.
Do you feel how the mountain swells?
Green and steep, it aches.
Do you see us in this class
pushing our ox hearts up the ridge
refusing to stop? Circle these chairs
now and tell the truth. Come on.

* * *

You borrowed my books
and returned them unread
and when you were murdered
I could not eat. All I saw
was your brilliant red hair
and the days you sat alone
in the back row, writing
those long apologies to me
for not writing your essays.

* * *

When I said to avoid all media
for two weeks, then rewrite again
I didn't intend that you should have
suddenly become a raving Christian.
Forgive me.

* * *

Tell me I was wrong about that
literary theft ten years ago? No,
no . . . It just took you ten years
to find out who the thief had been—
your roommate—who turned your rough
draft in. I didn't know. Thanks.

* * *

Are you the lost wagon train
who saw so much pure gold
that no one could find it again?
That could be your next story.
That could be your life. I know
many noble examples. So you have
a lot of experience. O.K. Tell me.

* * *

Don't ask me if you missed something
important. Don't ask me if you can be
absent. Your assignment is this: write
1,500 short sentences describing what
you think is important—for tomorrow.

* * *

You're angry about your grade. Well,
so am I. But not enough to erase it
or your magnificent mistakes, among
which I number this: "When they try
to apply this theory, the outcome
is usually fetal." So. Spit on your shoes.

* * *

Go from me now. I can only give you
words. Nothing's left except these:
    "I am alive, I am alive
     in this dark marsh
     by this wide field.
     Say my name, water.
     Say my name, willow.
     The teacher is gone
     The teacher is gone."
I will not answer my door. I will not.
See me next year, or ten, or fifty more.

Part III

Making Porridge

Hungry at forty for the slow flakes
take down the soft sack of Triangle Oats
measure out two cups as though you were
feeding work horses on a winter morning.
Run the old water into the cold pot
pinch the bright salt between your fingers
as your grandmothers did those thousands of years
then watch the worthy crystals settle, disappear.
The day's possible again. Water's on.

Wait. That curl of steam will rise—a genie
from the rounded steel. Loose your measured
whispering grain and watch it mound, settle,
darken, sink. Listen now. The crescendo
of the old Saxon mass begins: fast oaten
foam bulges, swells, rises, rebels,
and slides to its acrid end—scorched starch.
You turn everything down to simmer then
stir once with a wooden spoon.

Now, slow time comes. Setting out
the quart of milk and quart of honey, a bowl
and one bent steel spoon, you sit down.
Morning holds you still there, alone
at the round wood table. You see the oat
light over the Minam ridge begin to flame
and the mountains dark below, one ridge
the shape of a woman and children sleeping.
More wind shakes down more leaves

as you remember all the kitchens rich with
this same early light and calm
that time before anyone can speak or pray
before any terrible news is turned up high
before anyone can pass or spill the milk
before all the bowls are filled. There is
only this emptiness and this thickening sound—
the aubade of porridge, the hum of plain song.
Look outside now: the oatfield in November, 1984.

It volunteered green with fall rain
and even the stubble can't deny its affirmation—
that vote by grass for light. Remember the bowls
set before you: your family living on oatmeal
in Seattle in 1936 while your mother went to
university, and your grandfather fell timber in the camps;
your brother jobless in Spokane, married, living
on oatmeal when he crashed home from the Peace Corps;
your Scots grandfather eating only oats

and cream those years of Great Depression,
behind him centuries of oats on highland farms;
your wife unable to stomach the old staple
after your daughter was born. Now, this gold
bowl before you waits and everyone's asleep,
even the dog. Stir the old pot again
before it burns and remember that time
in Bellingham your mother, tired of picking up
rubber bands, served them to you and your brother

hidden in the morning cereal bowls.
When the water's penetrated to the hearts
and softened them enough for love, you pour out
the mass and inhale the steam, say ahhh and dip
your spoon into the honey jar and place
the sun in the center of this universe
and around the coasts you pour the cloudy milk
and wait for it to cool that first bite.
Goodness fills your mouth as the measured

simmered mass slides—yielding—inside you
and you tremble and begin to savor each grain.
As you eat slowly to the center, all the lives
in that kitchen come out to join you: a blonde
with bears and Oliver—wanting more—are first
and then the old ones—doctors, farmers, thieves,
pioneers—come and sit around you there
and watch you take in the simple sustenance
as they had done. Their empty mouths open

and close in rhythm with your steel spoon.
When your last bite's gone, they go out
like fires in the far marsh—starving for just
one taste of that sweet milk at the end
which you drink straight from the bowl—
against all the rules. Then you must rise—
leave the old pot stuck with nothing but truth—
and go out to the morning's chores—all that
mush banked inside you—

the pure energy of the poor.

❧

You Want to Go to Town?

That summer I was fired from the harvest crew, I had already been driving truck for about ten days, one of a crew of ten men who had been hired to harvest 3,000 acres of wheat in the Promise country of Eastern Oregon. The ranch was owned by the Mammons, a wealthy, town-dwelling family, but was worked by a tenant German immigrant couple, Helmut and Erma Berg. They were the heart of our crew: Erma cooked for all ten of us and Helmut fixed and serviced three combines, three grain trucks, and two crawler tractors. Nothing of any merit happened on that 3,000 acres without the Bergs, yet their story was part of what got me fired—an event I really didn't understand at the time, but still remember now, some twenty years later.

After ten days of being together, most of our crew had melded into a group of men who could laugh over mistakes, josh each other at meals, and tell stories in the bunkhouse after dinner. The two old transient headerpunchers, who had both worked for the Mammon family for years, kept to themselves. Sunburned, dried, hardened men, they took their thirst to town after dinner and often came back drunk at midnight or later, but were always ready to work the next morning. They were veterans of the western harvest circuit, both in their late fifties. In contrast, the catskinners were younger, usually jovial. They always took a teasing for falling asleep in the afternoons while their tractors were pulling the old green John Deere combines over the endless swales and flats of grain. Theirs was tedious work—all clank, dust, chaff, and diesel roar—and they often dozed off at the steering clutches. When that happened, the old headerpuncher would pelt the catskinner with a handful of wheat—another story. The other truckdrivers were schoolteachers—a common occupation in the summer for the local district employees. I was the youngest of the crew and had just finished my freshman year in college.

The only crew member who remained outside the circle of good will created by a harvest was Conrad—the youngest son of the Mammons. He slept by himself in an air-conditioned trailer in the shade of the locust trees behind Helmut and Erma's house. While the crew used the outhouse, washed in metal basins, and showered in a wood stall outside, Conrad used the house bathroom. He always sat at the end of the table at meals, as though he held a position of authority, but no one knew exactly what authority—if any—he held. He was tanned, soft-spoken, pious, and wore a new white clean tee shirt every day. His crew cut was Marine perfect, yet his hands seemed soft and feminine. His presence created a tension everywhere since we all knew that Helmut worked for Conrad's father and Helmut was clearly the man who knew the ranch and its machines. While I could have felt close to Conrad—he was the only person there my age—there was almost no talk between us. From the bunkhouse, we could see Conrad's light in his trailer and someone would say: "I wonder what he does out there by himself." "Probably got a lot of good magazines," someone would say, and the crew would laugh, then deal another round of poker.

Our bunkhouse—an old wooden building rank with sweaty socks, Bull Durham, Pinesol, and mouse-stained wallpaper—was so hot after dinner that often I would go across to the cooler open machine shop and spend my evenings helping Helmut sharpen sickles, replace sections, fix drapers, weld axles, grease machines, change oil—the infinity of work that he always had to do for the next day. It was here that I learned about local injustice from Helmut. For three years, he told me, he and Erma had been sponsored by the Mammons as immigrants and were living on their land and working for a small annual salary without bonuses or vacations. The inexorable routine of a dryland wheatranch had become a treadmill for them: weed, fertilize, seed, harvest, plow, disc, harrow, weed again. Harvest was the worst time, he told me. To keep up with cooking three huge meals a day for us, Erma had to hire a girl from town. Both Helmut and Erma felt that the hired girl's food and wages should be paid by the Mammons, but they had refused—even though many other wives in the community commonly hired girls to help them during harvest. Evidently, it was all right to pay extra men, but tenant women had to just work harder. Worst of all, Helmut told me about the meat—a symbol of good will and served at every meal. Whenever Mr. Mammon or one of his other sons came to visit us, the amount of prepackaged meat, ordered by the Mammons and delivered from town, stayed the same. Thus, someone in the kitchen had to go without meat, or else Helmut and Erma had to pay for extra meat themselves. They had asked the Mammons to add an extra chop, steak, or a few slices of bacon to the packages for the hired girl or for visitors, but the Mammoms had refused. All of this added up to Helmut and Erma feeling both angry and trapped. They could not protest too much because they feared the Mammons might send them back to Germany. They hoped to become U.S. citizens. Listening to Helmut's broken English-German as we worked together in the cooling shop, the wind rattling the metal roof and siding, I began to feel their injustice as though it were being done to me.

This was intolerable. Food at harvest was practically the sole agent of delight. Men working sunup to sundown six days a week, men sweating out 2 gallons of water a day in the 100-degree heat, men breathing grain chaff and powder-fine dust, men trying to keep complicated machines moving, men trying to live without women, men knowing their work was making a rich man richer—such men must *never* be able to complain about their food lest all that tenuous dignity and harmony generated by their common labor and wages be compromised. There always had to be more than enough food. Dishes always had to be hot and wellcooked. Food had to be hearty, wholesome, and traditional. Those meals—meat at every one—were the only delight available except our talk. For me, and for the other men, learning about the Mammons' miserly treatment of the Bergs had changed our view of meals. We ate, yes, but with qualifications: an eye on Conrad, an eye on the meat platter as it went around, an eye on Helmut and Erma, an eye on the hired girl. Now, I think that Conrad himself must have picked up this tension, but he said nothing—as usual—and kept his combine running. It was the only self-propelled, the only new machine.

All of this collided one July day—my last at the Mammons' ranch. One of the veteran headerpunchers, Old Bill, had spent the night in town drinking, but had come swerving back just after breakfast and pulled himself up on his combine. With a little liquid refreshment in his brown paper sack, Old Bill sat in the red morning sun ready to hit the field. He'd done this before, and the truckdrivers knew what to expect. Bill would be needing rest stops today—all day—so he wouldn't be flagging truckdrivers *before* his grain hopper was full. He'd wait until he was overflowing with wheat, then stop his machine, which would bring Conrad's wrath on the truckdrivers. A stopped combine was a big financial loss. We had to unload while the combine was moving. Old Bill was drunk and ready. He knew he could work his header, nip at his bottle, and fault the truckdrivers and he also knew we wouldn't say anything to Conrad or Helmut. A crew didn't make trouble for each other unless it was absolutely unavoidable. Everyone knew this and so did I.

At lunch, there was a lot of laughter among the crew at the sudden changes in the height of Old Bill's stubble, but Conrad was angry and before we left for the field he chewed me out for making Old Bill's combine stop. Of course, Conrad didn't know what was going on. No one would tell him that Bill had been in town all night. Bill hardly ever came to breakfast anyway. Conrad slept and washed by himself. I didn't like Conrad's attack on me and neither did the rest of the crew, but no one was going to tell Conrad that Old Bill was hitting more than the water jug at 10:00 a.m. We just let the tongue-lashing go. "Don't worry about what he says," Helmut told me. "You just keep that truck going." I didn't like what Conrad had done, yet I didn't confront him. I just took Old Bill's negligence on and heaped it with the other injustices I had already reaped from Conrad's treatment of Helmut and Erma. We went back to work as usual, moving as men do who have eaten a big lunch in a cool house—reluctantly, slowly, sleepily. The metal shop roof pinged loudly as the whole building swelled and shimmered in the 100-degree heat. The truck cab was an oven. One of the other truckdrivers had just touched his nose and it had begun to bleed. He would be late into the field.

After my second dusty trip to the elevator that afternoon, I saw Old Bill's combine stopped on the far side of the field. I roared over to him and unloaded him, then parked my truck and ran around his combine—all belts, shafts, huffs, and flails—climbed the steel steps to the deck. As I appeared, Old Bill tucked his bottle away, pulled down the brown bill of his baseball hat. I shouted to him over the roar of the combine: "Why don't you signal *before* you're full?" His face like an unshaven bulldog, brown wizened skin, his eyes bloodshot and glazed, Bill stared at me, smirked, and turned away. He was standing drunk and he loved it. "Why don't you signal?" I shouted again. I was a freshman then. I believed in my innocence. I was a good truckdriver, no matter what Conrad had said. Old Bill spat a brown streak of tobacco juice over the side, then started his reel and draper. His grain cylinder roared beneath us and grain dust filled my nostrils and eyes as he signaled the catskinner to roll ahead with a whirl of his hand. I jumped off his combine and ran back to my truck, not knowing that I had just broken a major but unspoken harvest rule: *truckdrivers never go up on the combines.*

After dinner, the thick dust on the road between house and bunkhouse was packed and shining where the crew had walked back and forth. I had showered and was laying on my hot bunk staring out the fly-specked window at the outhouse when Conrad came in. He'd never been in the bunkhouse before. He had an angry look on his face when he spoke to me: "I want to talk to you—outside." All the crew stopped talking and looked at Conrad, then at me. Harvest was nearly over. Maybe there were three days of cutting left. What could he want? I looked at him and didn't move. He was dressed in his usual white tee-shirt and jeans. So was I. It never occurred to me that I should be afraid of him or that he feared me. I was still angry about his attacks on me that afternoon. It never occurred to me that he was about to fire me. We went out the slouching screen door into the softening dusk and stood by an old combine header rusting in the yard.

"Bill says you went up on his machine today," Conrad said. There was a rising anger in his voice. I didn't know why.

"That's right," I said. "I thought he should be giving us more warning."

"But you went up on his machine," Conrad said. "Is that right?"

"He's causing the problem. Ask the crew," I said.

"That's none of your business," Conrad said.

"You mean I'm supposed to get chewed out by you for something that Bill's doing and not say anything about it?"

"I'm the boss here, not you," Conrad said. "You want to go to town?" He was angry now, and I honestly didn't know why. I wasn't ready for what came out next.

"If you're the boss, why don't you do something about the wages for the hired girl, and what about the amount of meat in the packages, and why don't you give Helmut and Erma a break once in a while? Shit." I was angry now too, but nearly crying.

"They've got nothing to do with you," he said.

"From what I hear, you aren't paying your share at all," I blurted.

"You want to go to town?" Conrad shouted at me. I didn't know what he meant.

"What for?" I shouted back.

"You want to go to town?" he shouted again. I still didn't know what was happening.

"You want to take me?" I shouted back. I wasn't going to give him the pleasure of hearing me say yes. Then, suddenly, I knew what he wanted—to fire me.

"Pack your stuff," he said. His upper lip was quivering and his fists were clenched and he was shaking. I was about the same. Now, I don't think he'd fired anyone before. I don't think he'd ever been in charge of a harvest crew and he knew he was barely in charge of this one. While his father had given him responsibility, Conrad really didn't know how to discharge it—except with me.

I went back into the bunkhouse and packed. It didn't take long—clothes, sleeping bag, shaving kit, a few novels. Some of the crew gathered around and watched me. I tried not to look at them. One asked me what had happened and I told him I'd just been fired for telling Old Bill to signal earlier. "Sometimes it's better to keep your mouth shut," Denny said. He was another truckdriver from Connell. I looked at him, grabbed my stuff, shook hands with everybody, and went out. Helmut had heard everything and came over. I said goodbye to him. Conrad pulled up in his big red Lincoln and stopped sharply in the dust. He had recruited the other headerpuncher to ride shotgun with him. I realized then that he was afraid of me. I got in the back seat and we roared away to town. There was a kind of ritual silence in the car which Conrad filled with the radio. We rolled fast and easy through the Oregon night, the car's headlights touching stubble along all the curving roads.

At the Greyhound depot in town, Conrad rapidly wrote out my check. Without thinking, I took out my wallet to put the check away, then suddenly remembered that I had found a fake badge with "Special Police" written on it in a Crackerjacks box. I suddenly felt the load of my own helplessness spill over me. I flipped my wallet open so Conrad could see the badge, then I quickly flipped it shut again, just as I'd seen detectives do on T.V. "You haven't heard the last of this," I said ominously, trying to keep a straight face. He looked quizzical and paused. "Special Police," I said, trying to sound mysterious. He stared at me a moment, then got in his red Lincoln and drove away. I laughed aloud and said, "You son of a bitch," then looked around at the warm night: the big moths were hitting at the yellow bulbs of the depot and I was free. I went in and bought a ticket home. Two hours to wait. I asked the ticket agent where the Mammons' $100,000 house was. Even he knew. I walked there and stared at its long brick facade. It looked neither expensive nor inviting, so I walked to the park and watched the swimmers and drank a cold 7-Up until it was time to go.

Later, I felt like I'd done something I should have, but wasn't sure I understood any of it. I knew I'd protected Old Bill because it was the crew's custom, then been fired—ostensibly—because I'd not known another custom that protected Old Bill even more. I also knew I'd come to feel more outrage than I could contain, yet that outrage was mostly for Helmut and Erma, and their condition, and they seemed the most important. I never understood any of this then, except that I felt as though I'd suddenly been unloaded because I had spoken. Now, I don't think Conrad had ever been in charge of a marble game. Conrad's father must have finally given him some responsibility, but he couldn't discharge it—except at me—and that as crudely as my efforts to be a responsible member of the crew.

〜

Out in the County

The barns are falling in rain
goats strain for quackgrass
on their chains in the mud yard
the old orchard goes unpruned
thickets and thickets
of chaotic apples bloom
small wormy abundance falls in tons
the moths learn to rule

Out in the county
the old logger dies in his bed
his wool quilt in rags
the yard fills with sudden cars
the neighbors come with meatloaf
come with red jello
for the widow and her dog
chicken feed spills on the cold porch
where crooked canes lean

Out in the county
rockjacks rot down to dirt
the teasel and tansy come on
morning glory crawls and covers
the haywagon, horse-drawn mower
windrow rake, manure-spreader
the last bull rusts in the pasture
his tail and hocks all matted with burdock
thistles ride the wind

Out in the county
something without hands
something huge, distant
keeps just the black roads to town
keeps the roads to the parks
the camper hookups, boat launches
garbage dumps, nice views open
patrolled, painted, sprayed, guarded, cleaned
while homesteads die according to law.

☙

Builds Strong Bodies Twelve Ways

"I said to leave the building."

"I was real thirsty."

"You got your drink. Now get out."

Eddie Latham's fists waited like knots in taut chain, hoping the principal would come down the stairs. He could smell the cornbread from the cafeteria. Carefully arranged pictures of graduating classes lined the walls above him—15 students one year, 20 the next. It wasn't a big high school. He looked down to the bulletin board. Heads of thumbtacks looked like steel eyes at the corners of the posters—blue and Navy, drab and Army, green and Marine. Always, the rifle, flag, ship, white gloves, smiling hard faces waited at the bottom of the stairs by the front door. Always, the poster people had their eyes poked out by someone with a sharp pencil who usually drew a mustache and sideburns on them so they looked like Elvis. Eddie heard the principal jingling his keys at the top of the stairs. Without looking up, Eddie could see his red face, black suit, white shirt, and bolo tie dangling below his triple chins. A real fatass.

"I'm going, I'm going," Eddie said. He backed slowly toward the door, clunking the horseshoe taps on his black leather boots on the polished and oiled wood floor. Too bad the principal wouldn't come down. Now, Eddie saw the coaches join the principal at the top of the stairs. They must have heard him shouting. He saw them mumble, laugh, look down—three chubby faces cut off at the necks by white collars. One held a grade book. From the bottom of the stairs, they looked tilted, and strange—all creased trousers and small heads. Eddie touched the cold brass curve of the door handle. It felt smooth, cold, solid—like a powersaw grip or a rifle stock. "See you later, fatass," he shouted up the stairs. He wanted everyone in study hall to hear. He flipped the finger, then backed out the doors into the cold February morning.

He sat in Grandys—the back booth next to the window—and ordered a cherry coke. When Mrs. Grandy brought it, he pulled out his wallet from his jeans and handed her a dollar, and asked for change for the jukebox. He hunched over the coke as though he were nursing a warming fire and watched as she shuffled back to the register. How many times had he seen her push those keys, watched the drawer slide out, heard the bell ring, seen the black/white numbers jump in the glass top. Maybe she would sit down and talk a while if she didn't have prescriptions to fill. The drugstore was warm. They could shoot the bull and he could watch out the window for a ride home. It was a good place to wait. She wouldn't make him feel like he had to leave. The black table top had his initials and thousands of others carved into it. Thousands of wads of gum were stuck to the bottom and no one worried about cleaning them off. If you didn't get too loud or come in drunk you could stay for hours. Mrs. Grandy stood by the table looking out the window.

"Out early today?" she said, handing him the quarters.

"Little bit; I got excused."

"What you gonna play?"

"You choose for me, Mrs. Grandy."

She smiled at Eddie and stood up and punched L-3. She always played that. "Sixteen Tons" was her favorite song. Looking straight at Mrs. Grandy, Eddie reached over and punched a couple of buttons, then laughed.

"What'd I get?" he asked her.

"'Crying In The Chapel' and 'Get a Job,'" she said, watching the machine move slowly, studying the records inside the clear cover that had lit up with his touch.

"Well, at least I didn't get 'Que Sera Sera,'" he laughed.

"God, I couldn't take that at this hour," she said.

He took a long drink of his red coke and she hummed along with her song, tapping her pink slippers softly, nodding her head with the chorus. She watched Eddie as he stirred the ice around in his glass with his straw, then watched him as he looked out the window. She knew him. He was like the others. No father, he grew up fast—tough, strong, solid, for his age. He'd been working in the woods for two years. His knuckles were big, raw, scarred, but his face was barely bearded and was soft in the light reflecting off of the melting snow. He had to act old, but was very young. She watched his brown eyes follow the Wonderbread man into the Lakeside Grocery across the street. "He's got a load today," Eddie said.

"You going back this afternoon?" she asked.

"Hatchetface told me not to come back."

"My daughter didn't have much use for him. I don't guess I know ten people in town who like him, but he's been up there so long nobody can get rid of him."

"I'm gonna make like an alligator and drag ass outta here."

"I know," she said. "Everybody will be out for lunch."

Eddie tipped up his coke all the way and left the glass half full of reddish ice. Something had happened to the boy, she could tell, but he wasn't going to tell her the story. They stood up together.

"What you going to do? Go to work for your uncle?"

"Don't know. Almost got killed up there last summer. You know what I mean?"

"Maybe you should try the mill. I don't like to see you just sitting around all winter." She stared out the window after his stare. He pushed himself up out of the booth before "Sixteen Tons" was over and started for the door. She followed him, listening to his heavy boots and horseshoe taps clank on the hard floor.

"What you want me to tell them?"

"You think of somethin', Mrs. Grandy."

He stopped at the cash register for a moment and looked at her face, her one gold tooth winking a kind of light at the corner of her mouth. He thought he should say goodbye to her or at least tell her what happened, but he couldn't now.

"How about I tell them a rich chick from Spokane picked you up?"

"Sure. In a candy-apple Corvette."

"And you won't be back for two years because she wants a long honeymoon."

"And a mink coat. I gotta go, Mrs. Grandy. Thanks for everything."

She watched him go down the drugstore aisle, spinning all the stools as he passed by them. He stopped to look at the new *Field and Stream* cover of a big buck in the mountains on a fall morning. Yes, he was like the others: boys from the farms and stumpranches around Clagstone or Edgemere, Athol or Belmont. They rode the busses two hours into high school in the morning, and two hours back at night. Sometimes they graduated, but most of the time they didn't. Some had to go to work, some to get married. Some had to choose between jail or the army. Eddie would be hard to predict. She thought of how they all started with milk in them, or formula she sold their mothers, then grew up to her cokes, and then beer. She could see it all mixing around inside of them. Mrs. Grandy was tired. Thinking of Eddie and all the boys she's seen like him made her tired. She wanted to go back to sleep. She went back and sat down at Eddie's coke in the back booth and watched out the window. She was thirsty. She picked up Eddie's coke and took a swallow of what he'd left. It was cold, red, and watery. She watched him as he talked to the Wonderbread driver across the street. "Builds Strong Bodies Twelve Ways" and red and blue polkadots on the side of the truck.

"I got to get home and the bus doesn't go until 3:30." Eddie turned up his denim jacket that was newer than his jeans, tucked in his red flannel shirt, tightened his black belt a notch. The February sun was just warm enough now to melt the slush everywhere. Main Street was a dirty melting mass of ice ruts and berms of shoveled snow. The Wonderbread man looked like a big bloodhound to Eddie. His eyes were saggy and red and he had puffy dark bags for cheeks.

"What you need?"

"I just got a call from my old lady. She says the water pipe busted."

"Why don't she call your old man?"

"Don't have an old man. She's home by herself."

"See that sign, kid? *No Riders.* Sorry."

Eddie kicked his black oiled work boot into a pile of slush and watched as the bread truck pulled out to go down to Sippert's Grocery. He headed for the highway. It wasn't a bad day to get kicked out. The sun was bright—too bright—and when he got to the highway, he started hitchhiking. The houses in town looked like cardboard boxes half buried by the snow that had slid off the metal roofs all winter. Plastic windows flapped in the slight wind. It was a lonely sound to him. Icicles dripping and falling from the eaves into the berms of snow like bones. At every house, a narrow trail was shoveled out to the highway and cut through the huge gravel-studded berms between which he walked.

The aroma of baking bread came to him from one house and he wanted to go in, but he kept walking until he passed the city limits sign, then stopped, took out his pocket knife, cleaned his nails, then put the knife away and waited. Toward Newport, the highway looked like a sheet of steel gleaming in the sun. A new Ford went by and sprayed slush on him. He cussed it, then kicked out a place in the berm where he could jump across if another car went by. He waited. Everything was melting and bright around him.

As he watched the highway toward town, Eddie saw the Wonderbread truck turn at the blinker light and start toward him. As it came closer, Eddie decided to put out his thumb just to see what would happen, just to make it a little worse for the Wonderbread man if he went past. He was just about ready to give him the finger when the truck slowed and stopped beyond him, the huge black tires and mudflaps dripping slush and water.

"I couldn't pick you up back there in town, kid. Rules is rules."

"How long you been drivin' bread truck?"

"Too damn long. Must be going on 25 years now."

"I set chokers a couple of summers."

"I'm starting to see bread in my sleep now."

"Why do you keep doin' it?"

"Oh, its better than a kick in the ass, as they say. Besides, I don't know what else I'd do. Say, you hungry, kid?"

"No. I just had a coke."

"There's some pastries in that box. Help yourself."

Eddie opened the box on the seat and looked in. A sour purplish smell rose from the small packages all heaped together, pushed down, broken open. Some of the wrappers were stuck to the frosting. Berry juice leaked out of the pies. After a minute, Eddie found a package of Snowballs that wasn't too badly smashed.

"You want one?"

"No, help yourself, kid. I don't eat that junk any more."

"I used to eat these for lunch every day."

They rode for a while, Eddie finishing off a couple of berry pies, and looking out the window and thinking how much better it was riding home with the Wonderbread man instead of riding the bus with all those screaming grade school kids. The heater under the dash warmed his toes. Pines along the road were dropping their snow loads. Suddenly, everything was bright. Eddie could hear road slush thudding on the undercarriage and see it spraying away from the tires in the rearview mirror. Whenever he looked over at the driver, he was holding the wheel in both hands and staring ahead, squinting against the light, a scowl on his face like someone had run a six-bottom plow across, then not harrowed it smooth.

"What you staring at, kid?"

"Just watchin' the flats for deer."

"You hunt the flats, do you?"

"Sometimes. I like to hunt up on Hoodoo better. I got my deer up there this fall. Where I was you could see clean over to Washington."

"Jesus, I haven't hunted for years, ever since I came back from the war. You about out of school?"

"Almost."

"If I was you, I'd get my service out of the way. It did wonders for my two boys. Straightened them right out."

"You take them huntin'?"

"Never did."

"See that mail box up there. That's my place."

"Let you off at the road, O.K.?"

"You goin' to Newport now?"

"Right. They've got it timed so I have to keep driving steady to get back by six. There you are, kid."

"Thanks for the ride." He jumped down out of the truck, his horseshoes on his boots making a loud whack on the wet blacktop. "Take it easy now."

"I'll take it any way I can get it." They both laughed, then Eddie slammed the door and watched the Wonderbread truck pull away.

As he walked toward the house, he tried to stay in the tracks that he'd walked in all winter, but wherever he stepped melting snow sank away and dropped him deeper. Even the heavy crust on the fields, which had once glistened so brightly that he could not look at it, had turned dull and flat now. He belched up a sourness and his belly started to turn queasy. He tried to swallow the sour taste but it hung there and burned in the back of his throat. On the front porch, dark glistening beads of water dripped from the eaves onto the porch planks in a steady rhythm. Eddie wiped his boots, his hand resting on the brittle curling shingles. A few more had blown away this winter in the heavy storms. He sometimes would find them twisting and spinning down the road like leaves driven between the two frozen berms.

He closed the front door, carefully, avoiding the loose panes of glass. The house was warm and smelled of roasting venison. His father's face stared at him from the mantle; his peaked khaki cap and two shining brass U.S. buttons on his lapels and his father smiling, the one who never came back from the war. Eddie stood listening, then crossed the frayed rug to his room. No sense telling her now. She'd just cry or something stupid like that and start saying things about how if his father was alive, and if this and if that—a lot of things he didn't want to hear. He heard a low groaning in the water pipes—she was in the kitchen. In his room, the smell of Hoppes solvent was heavy. He lay on his bed and tried to sleep but whenever he closed his eyes, he started to fall, his head spinning and tumbling around and around like it was a falling boulder rolled off a mountain. When he opened his eyes, green geraniums in red pots on the wallpaper blurred and moved. He lay there between delirium and dreaming, balancing his stomach like a warm uneasy bowl.

About three o'clock, Eddie got up and went quietly to the front door, opened it, then slammed it, rattling the glass, and called out, "I'm home." His mother came out of the kitchen wiping her hands on her apron, then stood—arms akimbo—in the dim room. She was a large gaunt woman with steel gray hair and a kind face.

"You don't have to lie to me, Eddie," she said. "I heard you come in the first time."

"I didn't do nothin', Mom. I was just—"

"You don't have to explain. Mr. Gaylord called and told me what happened." She stepped toward him. "Are you sick? You're white as a sheet."

"I could use some milk. My stomach's going ten directions." They went into the kitchen where the smell of roasting venison was rich and heavy in the air. She poured a tall cold glass for him, then set it on the table by the kitchen window where they always sat for prayer, meals, and Bible reading. The table was a clutter of letters, bills, and church papers.

"What'd you have for lunch?"

"Some pastries. The Wonderbread man give me a ride out."
He picked up the milk and took a long drink, leaving a white
mustache on his upper lip. He sat for a moment, then jumped and
ran. He could feel his belly churning and his mouth watering,
and he heaved himself down at the toilet, his belly tight like a
fist, then loosening, then tightening, Wonderbread dots rolling
in and out of his vision like hard steel bearings. When he felt he
was empty, he opened his eyes, flushed the toilet, and rinsed his
mouth with cold water and tried to get the taste out of himself
with toothpaste before he went back to the kitchen. She was
peeling potatoes at the sink.

"You feel better now? We're having venison roast for dinner."

"God, that's an awful taste," he said.

"Eddie, how many times have I asked you not to swear? Now,
your Uncle Robert wants you to come back setting chokers. He's
got some work for you around the mill until the roads are good
again. He'll pick you up at the highway at 6:30 in the morning."

"I don't wanta go back to work for him."

"You should have thought of that before you cussed Mr.
Gaylord."

"Aw, for Chrissake, it wasn't my fault."

"Eddie, please—"

"He was makin' fun of a hunting story I wrote, so I just
grabbed it away from him and told him to shove it."

"I don't want to hear any more about it, Eddie."

"Well, I'm not goin' back up there."

"What else can you do?"

"I don't know."

"Well, you've got to do something."

"I know. I know. You don't have to tell me that. Everybody's
been telling me that." He looked away out the window, staring at
the barn, the melting fields, the pines, and the rise of the ridges
into the dark horizon. He was quiet for a while. "I might join the
Marines." His mother turned quickly—as though she'd been hit
between the shoulderblades.

"Over my dead body. You better stick around here. Maybe you could get on with the railroad."

"I don't wanta be no gandy dancer. Besides, you have to know somebody to get on there. That's how Larry got on last summer."

"Well, you just better forget the Marines. First thing you know you'll get yourself killed. Then where would we be?" She turned to him with a sense of pleading, but he turned away. "I'm going out to gather the eggs before they freeze. You ought to lie down for a while. You're still white as a sheet. If you feel better, chop some kindling."

When his mother passed the broken willow into the low chicken coop, Eddie got up. He packed quickly, throwing in his hunting knife, frisco jeans, sweatshirt, alarm clock, razor, and socks and underwear. He grabbed a checkered wool coat out of his closet, threw it on over his blue denim. Downstairs, he looked in the breadbox but found nothing. He heard the venison roast popping and sizzling in the oven. He went to the oven door, hesitated, then came back and jerked it open. The blast of heat and the smell of meat roasting hit him in the face, but he reached in and pulled out the pan and set it on top of the stove. Grabbing a towel, he wrapped it around the haunch, then lifted it out of the pan. After wrapping the meat carefully in another towel, and tying it with some twine, he lurched out of the house and down the trail of now crusting snow to the highway, then down the highway until he was out of sight of the house.

No one came from Newport or Spirit Lake for a long time. No birds waited on fenceposts. It was quiet, cold, cobalt sky—empty and turning blackblue, a star hanging over the huge white hump of Hoodoo. Eddie Latham crouched beside the highway waiting between the two frozen berms of snow. They were freezing now. He shifted his weight from one leg to the other. His toes got colder inside his leather boots, and the end of his nose and his ears began to burn. Water stopped dripping everywhere in the woods along the highway and a thin sheet of ice began to glimmer on the blacktop. A pine squirrel sounded some place back in the timber. Maybe a buck was going under that tree now. Everything was getting gray. No one came. Eddie Latham wondered, as he stood waiting, wondered if he should take the roast back. Maybe it was only half-cooked. But he shot it and gutted it right up there on the mountain. It was his meat as much as it was hers, he decided. He could do what he wanted. He looked down at the roast lying on the suitcase. It was steaming slightly, as though it were breathing. He could eat that—if he had to. Someone would have to come soon. He would ride into Spokane and join. He thought of the roast then. What would he do with it? He didn't know. Suddenly from the north, he saw headlights come over the rise like two low stars. He would give the roast away to whoever stopped. The lights came on, pushing the gray night in front of them as though they were a great invisible blade on a plow carving out the space between berms. Eddie could see the yellow lights on the square box now, and the words "Builds Strong Bodies Twelve Ways" coming clearer. He still felt sick. Lights blinded him when he tried to look at them. He grabbed the suitcase and the roast, then stepped out on the edge of the road and waved the whitewrapped meat at the truck like a massive clenched and bandaged fist. He heard the engine slow, then pick up, the fan howling as the truck roared past him, the windblast almost knocking him down. Then, suddenly, he saw the brake lights flash red and the truck groan to a stop a hundred yards up the road. Eddie ran toward the lights, his suitcase and his kill heavy in his hands.

Conjuring a Basque Ghost

for Jean Ospital

You died as I could—
snag on the mind. I've fallen enough
timber to know how easy it is not to hear
that slight deadly crack in the top.
I know you didn't look up. The chainsaw roared
in your ears as you stood waiting like
a lamb while the widowmaker fell.

Three white horses graze your pasture now,
Jean Ospital. Your gates are locked, wife gone
to town, boys back in school two weeks after
the funeral. All your sheep are gone in steel
trucks. At your auction, everything sold high.
The realtor is out there now nailing up *For Sale*.

Do you want me to show how you loved your dogs
or drank the brown goat's milk? Should I say we
spoke in *Espanol* that day going down to buy
those five black fleeces still waiting here?
Should I say the ache in your eyes as you saw
the pasture dying in the heat, your ewes

grown thin? Should I put here your jeans
reeked with lanolin and sweat? Should I buy
your farm? I had no such money when the empty
trucks rolled in. What do you want from me?

Watching my wife spin the wool your dead hands
sheared, I make the little I know into this prayer
for you, Jean Ospital: *Pyrenees, receive*
this man. I send him home. Inside the mountain
that watched him being born, cover him
with wool and let him dream.

This is all I can say for you. *Adios, pastor.*
Leave me now. I have wood to cut today.

~

Part IV

Continuity in Northwest Literature

Contemporary commentators on regional literature in the Northwest generally assert that no identifiable regional literature has emerged in the country drained by the Snake, Columbia, and Fraser rivers. Writing in 1972, Robert Cantwell concluded that the recognized writers of the region do not "possess any sharply defined characteristics that identify them as belonging to the region." This view finds another spokesman in Richard Etulain, who states he cannot "find a group of writers in the Northwest whose writings reveal common characteristics which may be expressive of their regional background."[1] Similar statements have also been made by other writers and critics; although their arguments and evidence diverge, they all converge on the fact of an apparently amorphous literature.

At the same time that these writers and critics define their doubts about a regional literature, many of them also agree on a point which is generally touched only in passing. For instance, Cantwell's penultimate sentence reads: "It is possible that a new examination of the history of the old Oregon country will reveal that its overlooked educational power—the scenery—has been exercising its influence from the start." In his Preface to *Five Poets of the Pacific Northwest*[2] Robin Skelton writes that "the poets have all been deeply affected by their physical environment. It is obvious that, in this area, the landscape must have a powerful influence upon the art created within it." In a recent interview,

Richard Hugo, one of the poets included in Skelton's volume, states explicitly, "I think maybe in the Northwest poets there is a tendency to use more landscape . . . There's just less of the outside world gets into Eastern poetry."[3] If such statements are coupled with a reading of the writing about exploration and settlement, a study of Northwest poetry, and a cursory examination of Northwest literary history, it may be that environment and the human response to it will emerge as one source of continuity in the region's literature that cannot be easily dismissed. Although I am not yet prepared to say such a source of continuity is the distinctive characteristic of writing in the Northwest, I believe a survey of Northwest literature might describe a more continuous regional vision than writers and critics here previously claimed and might also serve to describe how a literature evolves under frontier conditions. In such an effort at survey, criticism, and synthesis, I believe I am following up on suggestions made by the contributors to *Northwest Harvest*[4], especially those of Harold G. Merriam in his paper "Does the Northwest Believe in Itself?"

I. 1781-1868

In this period, from the time of the first journal kept by a sea explorer describing the Oregon country up to the year of publication of Joaquin Miller's first collection of poems, most of the people who held pencils or pens in their hands in the Pacific Northwest were not what we would today call writers or poets. But what they wrote in journals, diaries, autobiographies, and letters constitutes what may be called a collective folk epic—not of going home, but of discovering, coming to, and settling in a new home. When read as a body, this literature is replete with *mythos*, heroes, a transcendent God, unknown country, dangerous terrain, mystical Indians, and hazardous passages. Read continuously for two weeks or a month, this literature constitutes a full document of "the mythic beginning," and what its writers chose and avoided can be seen as the roots for a future tradition.

Writers during the period of exploration and discovery, such as Robert Stewart, were generally charged with recording the physical facts of the region—flora, fauna, natives, weather, and terrain— and usually thought of themselves as wandering reporters or alien observers sojourning in the wilderness. Journey is their obvious form and ordeal in profane space is their frequent theme. The dominant tone in many writers is often a combination of gloom, nostalgia, and depression varied occasionally by writers like David Thompson and Theodore Winthrop, who celebrated the beauty of the Promised Land, and Simon Fraser and Alexander MacKenzie, who are both known for their sophisticated reporting. Generally, explorers moved through a new land they had to name and map, and most had neither the time nor the inclination to interpret or discover the spirit of the place or the people who inhabited it. Writers of Oregon Trail diaries and journals, another source of this collective folk epic, also focus most frequently on the facts of environment—how far they traveled, if they had water and grass, and where they were going tomorrow. A number of these writers also praise the fertility of the new land or mourn its desolation. Like many exploration journalists, emigrant diarists tend to be terse and do not investigate interior life. In general, they all report the physical details of wilderness that would allow themselves and others to orient themselves in the new space. Thus, the environment and their response to it—as something to be endured while it was discovered—became the major subject of these writers.

I believe we can claim that large body of original writing as a collective folk epic and see it as the beginning of a Northwest literature. The November 12, 1805, entry in the journal of William Clark illustrates the points I am making about form, subject, style, and tone, and demonstrates how accessible such prose still is today:

A Tremendious wind from the S.W. about 3oClock this morning with Lightineng and hard claps of Thunder, and Hail which Continued untill 6oClock a.m. when it became light for a Short time, then the heavens became suddenly darkened by a black cloud from the S.W. and rained with great violence until 12 oClock, the waves tremendious brakeing with great fury against the rocks and trees on which we were encamped. Our Situation is dangerous. we took the advantage of a low *tide* and moved our camp around a point to a Small wet bottom, at the Mouth of a Brook, which we had not observed when we came to this cove; for its being verry thick and obscured by drift trees and thick bushes. It would be distressing to See our Situation, all wet and colde our bedding also wet, (and the robes of the party which compose half our bedding is rotten and we are not in a Situation to supply their places) in a wet bottom scerecely large enough to contain us our baggage half a mile from us, and Canoes at the mercy of the waves, althou Secured as well as possible.[5]

To dismiss Clark's writing as simple historical artifact or to say that all this was simply written for Jefferson is to miss what it expresses about the human condition in new space: the environment was upon Clark and his men, even intimidating them. Clark wrote without specific names because he was not at home. He did not know what was out there, how it could be used, or how he and his men would have to change in order to survive. The diaries and journals of settlers show that in some cases men and women went mad under these conditions in which language, culture, and history had not yet established relationships between people and their environment that would allow them a greater chance of survival. Although the literal facts of such experiences seem to be their only significant dimension, what those facts *express* about the human condition in new space also needs to be understood.

This need to understand such writing on a symbolic level is particularly important because of the attraction of the folk epic to later novelists and poets who constantly return to it in much the same way that writers in other cultures constantly return to their epics and myths—as sources of expression for the true human condition at the origin, at *the beginning*. The presence of this epic in *Tale of Valor* by Vardis Fisher, *The Land is Bright* by Archie Binns, *The Big Sky* by A. B. Guthrie, *The Earthbreakers* by Ernest Haycox, *Swift Flows the River* by Nard Jones, and *Trask* by Don Berry—to name only a few novelists and novels—demonstrates that this epic is one of the most productive sources of recent Northwest literature. That contemporary poets in the Northwest have used two of the stances from this epic—the journal of traveling through unknown territory in search of sacred space as seen in William Stafford, and the autobiography of discovery in profane space as found in Richard Hugo—attests to its usefulness and durability.[6] The epic of people moving across unknown land and writing out their encounters with it continues in the books of such recent Northwest visitors as Edwin Way Teale in *Autumn Across America*, in Robert Cantwell's *The Hidden Northwest* and in the recently published journal titled *The Pacific Crest Trail*. Understood symbolically, the epic of discovering new space and the act of writing out the human response to that new space has defined and directed much of our literature.

II. 1868-1919

If the early collective folk epic shows that the environment and the human response to it were the requisite materials for writing in the region, what followed in this next period was an extended naming and cataloging of environment. Such an impulse, which found national expression in the poetry of Walt Whitman, was carried on with difficulty here because of a transplanted set of literary techniques and attitudes that allowed description and inventory of the new place to continue, but without any new perception of it. For instance, the Columbia "murmurs plaintively," the moon is a Queen, the sun is Venus, the west is purple. British topographical terms like *wold, mead, glen, dale* and *brae* appear throughout the poetry. Seas have breasts, rivers have silver tongues, brooks babble and winds whisper. Unlike their predecessors, who had probably not been reading the publications of the Hakluyt Society or exploration diaries, these writers were bound to a preconceived poetic vision that was designed to embody the facts of a settled agrarian territory.[7] Such a poetic vision could not encompass the environment and lives of settlers on a frontier where the Cayuse were still feared and where people were surrounded by millions of acres of wilderness.

Tied to such a preconceived vision, most poets could only write out their predictable jargon of an idyllic pastoral landscape and then try to find an audience for their poetry in places like London, where the British still believed in their own poetics, as Joaquin Miller did. But in the Northwest, I sense that no matter how many times Joaquin Miller wrote

As proud Columbia frets his shore
Of sombre, boundless wood and wold,
And lifts his yellow sands of gold
In plaintive murmurs evermore,[8]

and no matter how many times he described Oregon, "The Great Emerald Land" in these terms—

I heard their shouts like sounding hunter's horn,
The lowing herds made echoes far away[9]

—I doubt that anyone in the Northwest believed that such writing embodied the Northwest experience of environment. The terms and perceptions are clearly British, and we expect to see Squire Thomas Gray riding through the sagebrush after rattlesnakes and coyotes with his hounds. Juxtaposed with this entry from Robert Stewart's *On the Oregon Trail*, the contrast between pastoral England and the Northwest experience of wilderness is clear:

The sensations excited on this occasion and by the view of an unknown and untravelled wilderness are not such as arise in the artificial solitude of parks and gardens, for there one is apt to indulge in a flattering notion of self-sufficiency, as well as a placid indulgence of voluntary delusions; where as the phantoms which haunt a desert are want, misery, and danger, the evils of dereliction rush upon the mind; man is made unwilling acquainted with his own weaknesses, and meditation shows him only how little he can sustain and how little he can perform.[10]

In the first two periods of Northwest literature writers made the environment and their response to it their recurring subject. While the writers of the collective epic were creating the first verbal maps of new space, the first generation writers could not, basically, front the facts of wilderness frontier experience in language. Instead of deriving their language from the environment confronting them, they took language, imagery, and vision from the historical poetic tradition of a settled country. The inability of that tradition to embody the Northwest experience of and response to environment was intensified by an even greater inadequacy in the Genesis *mythos* which separated people from their environment.[11] Coming to new space without a "mythology that married us to rock and hill" (as Yeats said it in *The Trembling Veil*), first generation writers brought instead a mythology that declared our divine right to exploit, conquer, and subdue the environment and the people in it for exclusively human purposes. While the writers of the folk epic could focus on the physical facts of new space, the first generation writer had not only to continue to map and inventory but also to interpret that space in order to be at home in it. With only a mythology of conquest and without a language of terrain or a tradition that could embody wilderness frontier experience, they could only grope backward for British terms, Greek and Roman gods and goddesses, and a pastoral tradition.[12]

III.   1919-1946

In 1919, H. G. Merriam at the University of Montana founded what began as a campus periodical but later became the first major Northwestern regional magazine, *The Frontier*; in Portland in 1923, Colonel E. Hofer founded *The Lariat*. As *The Lariat*'s patron and editor, Hofer described his magazine's mission:

The Lariat might be called a volunteer captain in the lists of literary militancy. The fight is for undenatured nourishment to the popular mind, that the "conscience of the people" may be such as a free country may depend on. The past decade has been one of political and literary swindle. Hot air has been blown into everything, giving distention and inflation to every living avenue. A people with a conscience will react against this, and safety to the world of common good (not democracy) depends on how large a percent of the thinking humans are thinking for truth and beauty and brotherhood.[13]

In his editorial for the first regional issue of his magazine (1927), Merriam articulated the vision that he brought to the editorship of *The Frontier* for nearly twenty years:

The Northwest is industrially alive and agriculturally alive; it needs to show itself spiritually alive. Culturally, it has too long accepted uncourageous, unindigenous "literary" expression of writers too spiritually imitative and too uninspired. We in this territory need to realize that . . . the roots for literature among us should be in our own rocky ground, not in Greenwich Village dirt or Mid-west loam.[14]

These two magazines and their contrasting editors and editorial policies embody the continuing tension between the collective epic and the transplanted poetic vision. In contrast with *The Lariat*'s uncritical publication of anything that seemed "poetic," Merriam could not accept a poetry in which the preconceived vision of environment was dominant, and his editorial clearly expresses his opposition to the tradition of mimicry and easy pastoralism.

However, certain changes soon began to occur, as a reading of Merriam's 1931 anthology will show. Most of the old Briticisms for terrain have been replaced by more concrete local language. Black bears, lupin, sagebrush, hop-vines, moose, seagulls, crows—these and other similar nouns appear consistently in *Northwest Verse.* And the babbling brooks and murmuring rivers, the hunting horns and kings and queens have disappeared. Although the movement away from the transplanted tradition has begun, most of the poems in the anthology still only describe environment. In fact, Merriam declares in his Preface that he was overrun with poems that were descriptive "especially of the sea and of the sky with the sun and moon and stars and clouds." Thus, the style and language has begun to change, creating a kind of hybrid of the folk epic's language of immediate experience of environment written in the prosody of the transplanted vision which found such popularity in Portland.

But two writers who had grown up in the region were impatient with this hybrid and the dominance of the first generation tradition of mere description in pretty phrases. H. L. Davis and James Stevens blasted that imported tradition in their 1927 pamphlet, *Status Rerum,* which begins in this rhetorical fashion:

The present condition of literature in the Northwest has been mentioned apologetically too long. Something is wrong with Northwest literature. It is time people were bestirring themselves to find out what it is . . . . Is there something about the climate, or the soil which inspires people to write tripe? Is there some occult influence which catches them young, shapes them to be instruments out of which tripe, and nothing but tripe, may issue?[15]

In a later issue of *The Frontier,* Davis identifies in a guest editorial the problem's source more succinctly: "We began here with a new way of life, new rhythms, new occupations. We have failed to make that freshness part of ourselves." (By extension this applies, of course, to the environment remaining outside the language of poetry and fiction.) James Stevens also blasts the literary establishment of *The Lariat* in a scathing satirical article published in *The American Mercury* in 1929. His objections to *The Lariat* are formidable, but most of his attack is aimed at the poetic practices of mere description of environment, and frivolous or trite treatment of it, literary practices that do not join people and the space around them. Stevens illustrates the discontinuity among language, experience, and environment by writing about his first reading of the magazine:

My first encounter with the *Lariat* occurred when I was laboring on the green chain of the sawmill at Westport, Oregon. I was on the night shift, which ended at three in the morning. At the end of one night of labor, when a wet wind hammering up from the Columbia River bar had made work under the open shed of the green chain an infernal misery, I discovered a copy of the *Lariat* in a chair of the hotel lobby . . . As I gnawed my plug for a heartening chew, I idly turned the pages of the pretty publication.

Stevens finds the following poem by Col. E. Hofer, "Madonna of the Poor"—

She ne'er beheld the birth of day,
Or saw the infant morn born softly forth
On noiseless pinions of the air,
Laid in the pearly shell of dawn
And carried joyous on the shoulders of the sun.
She ne'er lived through a radiant day
When all the earth with feeling thrills
Beneath caresses of her lover bold . . .

—and writes: "I quit there, partly because I felt myself blushing, but mainly because I had swallowed my chew."[16] In both style and statement, Stevens shows how clearly language, experience, and environment did not meet, as earlier they had not met in Joaquin Miller and others. The facts of weather and work built into Steven's language instead echo the language of the folk epic and make the poem seem silly and affected.

The impatience of H. L. Davis with the poetry and standards of *The Lariat* is easier to understand when juxtaposed with his own poetry because this shows clearly a new relationship with and response to environment in Northwest literature. His poem "The Rain Crow" illustrates his advance:

While women were still talking near this dead friend,
I came out into a field, where evergreen berry vines
Grew over an old fence; with rain on their leaves;
And would not have thought of her death, except for a few
Low sheltered berry leaves: I believed the rain
Could not reach them; but it rained on them every one.
So when we thought this friend safest and most kind,
Resetting young plants against winter, it was she
Must come to be a dead body. And to think
That she knew so much, and not that she would die!
Not that most simple thing—for her hands, or her eyes.

Dead. There were prints in the soft spaded ground
Which her knees made when she dug her tender plants.
Above the berry leaves the black garden and all the land
Steamed with rain like a winded horse, appeared strong.
And the rain-crow's voice, which we took for a sign of rain,
Began like a little bell striking the leaves.
So I sat listening to this bird's voice,

And thought that our friend's mouth now, its "Dead, I am dead,"
Was like the rain-crow sounding during the rain:
As if rain were a thing none of us had ever seen.[17]

Like many of Davis's poems, which began to appear in *The Frontier* shortly after it was founded, "The Rain Crow" begins with environment, as did the collective epic. But Davis then moves beyond mere description; rain, berry leaves, crows allow the poet to objectify in language the experience of human life and death in an immediate locale. Such writing becomes possible when the poet has internalized environment, taken it as part of himself, and watches and listens and feels for the truth it expresses about the spirit of place, the moment, and the people. The image of mortality is fresh and the language is fresh because Davis is willing to name and name again and again; thus through environment he becomes articulate. His language touches the place because the place has been taken personally. It is fair to state that Davis's poetry shows, for the first time in the Northwest since the folk epic, that naming is more than mapping an external environment; such externals are also a means of binding environment to the internal universe of human experience.

In fact, Davis is the first Northwest poet literally to pack his poems with local nouns as he does in these lines from "After Love":

Here I would invent praise, and have learned no other than to name
the kinds of grass here: the great bunches of blue
windflowers that leak shining water; big-stemmed vetch;
yellow and black snapdragons; wild strawberry runners;
Cheat-and-ribgrass with white pollen rimming its dark heads

. . . .

And I am not ashamed praising by count this grass standing in the wind.[18]

As Gertrude Stein has said about other writers, Davis was "drunk with nouns." Having learned how "to name earth sea and sky and all that was in them was enough to make him live and love in names, and that is what poetry is it is a state of knowing and feeling a name," and by extension, a place. This immediate and specific unity of poet, environment, and language is the dominant presence in Davis's poems. By saying these names, Davis is showing us what *The Lariat* poets could not show us— that he had seen the Northwest and touched it with language that would make it possible to interpret human experience in new space.

In *The Frontier* and the writing of H. L. Davis and James Stevens, it is again clear that environment and the human response to it were the sources and materials for literature, while in *The Lariat* it is clear that the sources and materials for literature were the conventions of an imported literary tradition. This tension between the folk epic and the transplanted vision fostered numerous literary quarrels, and I understand that the repercussions of *Status Rerum* are still audible today in certain circles. Certainly, the imported tradition can still be found among the newspaper column poets and various local and state poetry societies, and also, no doubt, in schools and colleges. But the larger disagreement between the two magazines arises here quite clearly. In response to the most demanding questions of our literature—"Where are we?" and "How shall we live here?"—*The Lariat*'s reply was basically to perpetuate and even exaggerate a poetic tradition of people separated from environment and bound exclusively to a historical past. In contrast, *The Frontier* responded by advocating a literature that would unite people and environment through a language of the new place.

IV. 1946-present

With the arrival of four new literary immigrants between 1947 and 1949—Theodore Roethke, William Stafford, Leslie Fiedler, and Bernard Malamud—these questions and the continuous and conflicting answers to them were more sharply defined. In the pre-Northwest poems of Theodore Roethke, his affinity for the tradition of Davis, Stevens, and Merriam is stated quite explicitly. For instance, these lines in "Feud"—

There's canker at the root, your seed
Denies the blessing of the sun,
the light essential to your need.
Your hopes are murdered and undone.[19]

—articulate Roethke's consciousness of the inadequate *mythos* of a people separated from their environment and trying to be at home by conquest alone. He resolves this dispute personally in another pre-Northwest poem, "In Praise of Prairie," with these final lines:

Here distance is familiar as a friend.
The feud we kept with space comes to an end.[20]

This, I believe, declares a posture where subject and object co-alesce as they had in some of the poems of H. L. Davis.

William Stafford's alignment with Davis, Merriam, and Stevens is built into many statements and poems, but his most recent published statement on how the material for art and unity with self and place emerge appears in an article, "Having Become a Writer: Some Reflections":

The world was conspiring to teach me the lesson that is upon us now in the current literary scene: a new poem or story or novel or play can be traced back through earlier poems etc., and endless games can be played with analyses of influences from literature; but the plain truth of the matter is that any literary work must rely for its effects on bonuses and reverberations that derive from the original resonance between human beings and their total experience, not from that little special tangent that comes from the Literary Succession . . . the way toward a fuller life in the arts must come by way of each person's daily experience. To deny that experience—even to veer from it in a minor way—is a false step.[21]

This is the kind of statement that H. H. Merriam was making throughout his nineteen-year editorship of *The Frontier* and also the kind of statement, setting aside the pamphleteer's rhetoric, that Davis and Stevens were making in *Status Rerum*. This conflu-ence of Stafford and Roethke with *The Frontier*, Davis, and Stevens, all favoring what Stafford himself had earlier called "an immedi-ate relation to felt life" was an important contribution because it made the sources of mature art more local—hence more universal—and moved attentive regional writers even further from the traditions of Colonel Hofer and *The Lariat.*

In contrast with Stafford. and Roethke, Leslie Fiedler and Bernard Malamud acted out in both criticism and fiction the most recent statements of the very *mythos*—that we are bound only to human history, not to place—that *The Frontier* had challenged. In his essays on Montana, Leslie Fiedler more or less declared his condescension to the Northwest by assuming that local philistines could not see the mountains because of the movies, and we could not see ourselves except in Rousseau's mirror. (It was this kind of critical stance that later prompted W. H. Auden to note that Fiedler had no sense of landscape.)

In Malamud's *A New Life,* we see Levin's inability to respond to the environment or engage it in any significant way as the mark of his non-Northwest status and his derivation from homocentric *mythos* that could not include human unity with environment as part of its ethical structure. Levin's preoccupation with an exclusively human world exemplifies the tradition later Northwest writers have explicitly rejected, as may be seen in the work of Gary Snyder, who is the direct antithesis of Levin. It is a hallmark of Malamud's artistic acuity that he could see that even in Corvallis in the 1950s the major drama was not exclusively human. Even though *A New Life* cannot address the spatial and environmental questions that concern Gary Snyder, the novel remains an excellent description of what might be a developing distinctive quality in Northwest literature—namely, that literary material cannot be derived here from exclusively human relationships in time; our literature must also include the presence and influence of space and our responses to it.

It is also important to recognize that Roethke and Stafford both inherited a territory and a milieu from Davis, Stevens, and Merriam where the need for new teachers who could bring memorable language and local environment together had been expressed. It should be remembered that the second prong of the attack in *Status Rerum* was made against teachers of poetry and fiction in the regional universities who had been drawn into supporting the transplanted vision and who even encouraged writers to imitate the hack western and grind out the "snowflake school" poem. By example and by emphasis on technique, Roethke unknowingly provided what Davis and Stevens had described as lacking twenty years earlier. And the work of William Stafford in regional writers' conferences continues to provide a similar contribution. Walter Van Tilburg Clark and Vardis Fisher offered comparable, three-dimensional teaching at the University of Montana during the years they were in residence there, and the Rocky Mountain Writers' Conference and the University of Washington Writers' Conferences initiated by Roethke began to fill that pedagogical void. There was substantial confluence between the conditions of regional poetry and culture and the arrival of Stafford and Roethke. I doubt, however, that the same case could be made for either Fiedler or Malamud, although their influence also has been continuous as both poets and teachers.

Although I can describe only a small part of Theodore Roethke's contribution to Northwest literature—Richard Hugo and John Haislip have written excellent articles on this subject already[22]—I want to declare briefly what I believe his contributions were to this continuous tradition of making the environment and the human response to it the recurring subject of Northwest literature. His first contribution—that language is a means to unity with place—is fully articulated in his poem "The Rose" (1964) which begins:

There are those to whom place is unimportant,
But this place, where sea and fresh water meet,
Is important—
Where the hawks sway out into the wind,
Without a single wingbeat,
And eagles sail low over the fir trees,
And the gulls cry against the crows
In the curved harbors,
And the tide rises up against the grass
Nibbled by sheep and rabbits.[23]

To place this poem in a Northwest context, I want also to quote an
H. L. Davis poem from *Proud Riders* (1942) which opens in nearly
the same way on a comparable scene:

New Birds
Now all of the snow's gone from the high desert, now the frost
Lets go of the ground in the deep draws, we find
And recognize and enumerate new birds.
The blue bird's the first comer back to the dead grass range.
Out of some waterless gray rock-break, his low voice
Utters a song almost tuneless; but his blue wings
Are bright like gay innocent music. The brown thrush,
Colored like old hay weathered in the rain, then sings
At evening, when all's darkened except water. Then concealed
Among dark pastures of the desert, he sings his hurt.
The loud-voiced little yellow-hammers shine by day,
The color of new sagebrush blossoms. Red-winged blackbirds
Blazing at the wing-joints with scarlet like the blaze
Of naked red willows in the black creek-beds, flock and talk.
The thorn-brush jolts with hundreds of bright black-bodied
Birds joking over their new country. Then come swans.
Dark wild swans come from the cane marshes in the south,
And pass, long-throated and still-mouthed. Then white geese
Trail, reaching across the dark sky, broad-winged as eagles
But flapping their broad wings. Silence follows them.
No other new birds follow after these.

Both poets have perceived the function of naming as a means of
establishing unity with place; the place is important, must be
seen, and is a means to metaphor. For Davis, the return of spring
birds creates a mood of qualified hope, while for Roethke, the
scene begins to engage him at the beginning of his journey out of
himself. Davis's opening lines are not indicative of his subsequent
intention or mood, while Roethke's are indicative, and Davis
seems to be much more interested in the process of naming
(getting the names right) while Roethke seems to be interested in
both the external objects and the music of the language which
names them. As the poems develop, Roethke continues another
full stanza of naming shore birds while Davis introduces a contrasting stanza about birds that have wintered over on the high

desert. In the third stanza, Roethke opens with his second statement—"I sway outside myself / Into the darkening current." —thus intensifying his impulse toward unity with environment through naming the external landscape. In the same pivotal, transitional position, Davis says of the winter birds, "Without their presences,/ I'd have been too lonely to live on this bare plain." Roethke then continues to catalogue and expand the dramatic confluence between poet and environment for some ten additional stanzas until, in the fourth section, he comes to the end of swaying and articulates his unity with place:

Near this rose, in this grove of sun-patched, wind warped madronas,
Among the half-dead trees, I came upon the true ease of myself,
As if another man appeared out of the depths of my being,
And I stood outside myself,
Beyond becoming and perishing,
A something wholly other,
As if I swayed out of the wildest wave alive,
And yet was still.
And I rejoiced in being what I was:
In the lilac change, the white reptilian calm,
In the bird beyond the bough, the single one
With all the air to greet him as he flies,
The dolphin rising from the darkening waves;
And in this rose, this rose in the sea-wind,
Rooted in stone, keeping the whole of light,
Gathering to itself sound and silence—
Mine and the sea-wind's.

To this point, it would appear that, with the exception of attention to music in the language, there is an appealing similarity. Naming of the environment has led Roethke to transcendence in the same way that winter birds have led Davis away from self-consciousness and loneliness during the bleak winter. But the comparison ends there because Davis continues for another five lines of simile that apply his catalog of new and old birds to an unidentified woman:

It is the same with my beloved as with new birds.
Old thoughts, that were my company when I lived alone,

Under her beauty's and youth's energy, have been lost.
I strive to recover them, to put them all in words,
Thinking they'll help me again, when she is gone.[24]

What began years apart in the Northwest as a similar act of naming the external environment, and what appears to be leading both poets to unity with environment, has suddenly turned dissimilar with Davis's ending. While Roethke's ending expands, intensifies, and dramatizes his achievement of unity with place, Davis spins off into abstractions and rhetoric that close off possibilities of transcendence, exclude the reader from the poem, tack on a new question of interior life, and reduce the catalog of birds to a simple comparison. Although Davis has carefully attended to the environment and its names and has achieved a kind of metaphor with the first two stanzas, he is unable to bring together interior landscape and the exterior environment in his ending. In Davis's best poems, like "The Rain Cow," he shows he is capable of binding together people, environment, and language throughout the poem, but he was unable to achieve that unity here because he could not bring his entire internal life to the entire poem. When "New Birds" gets too self-revealing, Davis pulls back and the voice goes soft. For Roethke, the poet of "Open House," moving back was impossible. Instead, he simply moves more and more into the music of names, the voice remains strong, and he becomes what is around him.

I hope this comparison illustrates Roethke's first as well as his second contribution. While his language becomes the obvious means of unity with environment, Roethke also shows that external landscape must be balanced with attention to internal landscape if the poem is to avoid collapsing on itself. This was a major contribution to a developing literature that was still, by and large, dwelling on the physical and external details of environment as the writers of the folk epic had done. For example, the following poems, one by Roethke's predecessor at the University of Washington and one by a Montana poet, show the prominence of the descriptive tradition with the removed poet's voice reporting.

Philipsburg
An old man lives in a little grey town
Where, in his dreams as night slips down,
Creaking ore carts laden high
And strings of dusty mules go by
And men who heard the outlands cry.
But dreams grow pale in the morning sun,
And memories vanish—one by one.[25]

John Frohlicher

from *Rain on Orcas*
Rain in the islands,
With the black clouds flying,
And the last faint spots of sunlight fading on the sea.
Changing, hurrying, shifting of shadows,
And the high grey fan of rain-streaks in the east.

Darker, darker,
With the wind rising and falling more loudly in the trees,
The waves' slap sounding stronger and quicker on the sand,
Where the driftwood,
Sad, spent, weather-weary travelers of the deep
Lie grimly, white and naked to the rain
When it shall come.[26]

Glenn Hughes

Although both poems are clearly attempting to move beyond the language and posture of the folk epic, neither seems to escape it and achieve any unity between external and internal space. I believe this consistent dominance of "setting" or "nature" is less a result of an impoverished imagination than a result of, first, an intimidating physical environment; second, an inadequate *mythos* of space; and finally, an inadequate poetic tradition. Hence, writers could only describe unless they, like Davis, and now Roethke, interiorized environment and brought to it their full internal landscape.

This emphasis on the necessity of internal landscape in the poem—on a voice that would not go soft, merely descriptive, or abstract when confronted with environment—was also a major contribution to future Northwest writers (I think here of Richard

Hugo and David Wagoner) because it freed them from the dead-fall of a strictly physical poetry and made them intensely conscious of the importance of *voice* as the binding and significant presence in a Northwest poem. Although this contribution has not been acknowledged, I believe that the first books by both poets show the influence of this contribution. From *A Run of Jacks* to *What Thou Lovest Well Remains American,* Richard Hugo shows that equal attention to the music of language and to interior life are the only means of escaping tedium and inertness in a poetry where place and the naming of place and thing are the means of objectifying and discovering personal interior. Even though his experience in profane space may be gray, rainlocked, and desperate, the presence of Hugo's shaping, strong, musical voice carries the poems and the poet through the journey to another temporary stay against confusion. Although David Wagoner's vision is generally less bleak and more charged with intellect, Wagoner is often taking the task of animating a universe through voice alone, as can be seen in a poem like "Guide to Dungeness Spit."[27] It is possible that both of these poets, and others whose work I do not know, have learned the balance that Roethke taught between environment, interior landscape, and music. Instead of simply describing or feuding with environment in a *mythos* of detachment and conquest, Roethke showed future writers how articulate they could become if they simply united themselves with the space around them in a balanced fashion. To see how dramatically this has transformed Northwest poetry, compare Hugo's "Degrees of Gray in Philipsburg" from *The Lady in Kickinghorse Reservoir* with the poem about Philipsburg by John Frohlicher. The differences between them are attributable, in part, to the example of Theodore Roethke.

In the poetry of William Stafford we can see a final expression of the continuity in Northwest writing. Although there is much more to Stafford's poems than can be discussed here, the poems do generate responses to those two enduring questions of Northwest literature. To the question, "Where are we?", Stafford's reply seems to be that we have come to and are still traveling through a territory (both literal and metaphoric) where we must engage in the continuous act of discovering the unknown. Like the writers of the folk epic of discovery, Stafford sends back messages to Kansas and the East, makes reports on Oregon, writes many poems about traveling while he develops the ability to "hear the wilderness listen." His means to such a continuous process of discovery is articulated through environment in many poems; "Starting With Little Things" seems to illustrate how he proceeds:

Love the earth like a mole,
fur-near. Near-sighted
hold close the clods,
their fine print headlines.
Pat them with soft hands—

But spades, but pink and loving; they
break rock, nudge giants aside,
affable plow.
Fields are to touch:
each day nuzzle your way.

Tomorrow the world.[28]

Taking the perspective of the mole and binding it to himself, Stafford can articulate his unwillingness to abstract or generalize his love for new space. To be at home here, Stafford seems to say, we must establish a comparable immediate and personal unity with environment, as he has through the mole, through acts of the imagination that bridge with language and *mythos* the easy (or most difficult) barriers we have erected to separate people and environment. Instead of thinking of the environment as an exclusive arena for people and their work with machines, Stafford asks us to consider the mole's relationships to the environment where "Fields are to touch" and where clods have headlines we probably can't read because we haven't looked at their "fine print." In short, Stafford's voice encourages us to see the potential power in a vision that includes the nonhuman.

In contrast with Theodore Roethke, who dramatized his journey out of himself in "The Rose," Stafford begins many of his poems where "The Rose" ends. With his nearly *a priori* imaginative achievement of unity with environment, Stafford accomplishes in the first three lines of "From Eastern Oregon" what Roethke dramatized for the entire poem:

Your day self shimmers at the mouth of a desert cave;
then you leave the world's problem and find
your own kind of light at the pool that glows far back
where the eye says it is dark. On the cave wall
you make not a shadow but a brightness; and you can feel
with your hands the carved story now forgotten or ignored
     by the outside, obvious mountains.

Your eyes an owl, your skin a new part of the earth,
you let obsidian flakes in the dust discover your feet
while somewhere drops of water tell a rock.
You climb out again and, consumed by light, shimmer
full contemporary being, but so thin your bones
register a skeleton along the rocks like
an intense, interior diamond.

You carry the cave home, past Black Butte,
along the Santiam. The whole state
rides deep, and the swell of knowing it makes
yearning kelp of all you can't see.
For days your friends will be juniper, but
never again will material exist enough, clear—
     not any day, not here.[29]

Although I hesitate to explicate what has already been said so well, Stafford seems to be building into this poem one of his replies to the second enduring question of our literature—namely, "How shall we live here?" First, it is obvious that we must move beyond a literally reported, surface realism universe; we must move beyond the pretty descriptions of *The Lariat*. Even though he is nearly uninterested in the "outside, obvious mountains" of external landscape, and even though he states that surface material will never "exist enough" after this kind of encounter, his language is still the language of place as we saw it first appear in the folk epic and later emerge in the poetry of H. L. Davis. Like

Davis, Stafford's perceptions in the poem are gained through the eyes of an owl, and the cave is a place that must be perceived through this medium because so much of what its darkness contains is not available to the human eye. After such an encounter with place, the poet interiorizes it ("You carry that cave home"), and that act of becoming what was around him literally transforms his entire perceptual process and himself as well. All this suggests Stafford's reply is that we must "live by imagination," our only means out of the shimmering homocentric consciousness to unity with places inside and out of ourselves. Such unity replaces the need to simply and superficially describe, dominate, or conquer the cave; in fact, the cave itself becomes a means to a celebration and illumination of both the resources of environment and the imagination's ability to respond to environments it discovers or creates. If the imagination can separate people from environment and declare all life as subservient to human will, the imagination as Stafford shows can also restore people to a place within environment and document the *genius loci* of desert caves.

Although this analysis and survey of Northwest literature ends here, it is clear that the process needs to continue, since a great many excellent writers and poets—Vi Gale, Vern Rutsala, Kenneth Hanson, David Wagoner, Robin Skelton, John Haislip, Henry Carlile, Gary Snyder, Don Berry, Ken Kesey, William Kittredge, Madeline DeFrees, Vardis Fisher—need to be present in any complete study of Northwest writing. The absence of such writers and poets here makes it clear that a complete literary history of the Pacific Northwest needs to find an author. Such a literary historian would be obligated to trace other sources of continuity in our literature which have been omitted here: the presence of the Indian, the experience of women, regional magazines and presses, regional folklore, the influence of the universities, Northwest expatriates, the current literary situation, and so on. For such a history to be complete, it would have to include an analysis of that interface between environment and literature which, as I have tried to show, has become an obligatory locale, perhaps a unique territory, for Northwest writers and poets.

Notes

1. Robert Cantwell, *The Hidden Northwest* (Philadelphia: Lippincott, 1972), pp. 280-281; Richard W. Etulain, Comment on "A Symposium: The Pacific Northwest as a Cultural Region," by Raymond D. Gastil, *Pacific Northwest Quarterly*, 64 (October 1973), 159.

2. *Five Poets of the Pacific Northwest*, edited by Robin Skelton. Seattle: University of Washington Press, 1964.

3. William Stafford and Richard Hugo, "The Third Time the World Happens," *Northwest Review*, 13, No. 3 (1973), 43.

4. *Northwest Harvest*, edited by V. L. O. Chittick. New York: Macmillan, 1948.

5. *The Journals of Lewis and Clark*, edited by Bernard DeVoto (Boston: Houghton-Mifflin, 1953), p. 282.

6. In my essay, "The Search for Sacred Space in Western American Literature," *Portland Review*, 22, (1976), 6, I define *sacred space* as "implying home, a heterogeneous landscape in which man has both privileges and responsibilities. It contains enduring qualitative differences. It has fixed points, centers, from which all human activity takes its meaning. It endures beyond any particular individual as a source of objective reality. In sacred space, there is continuity between internal and external space; man seeks that continuity and binds himself to it. He claims space as part of himself, he identifies with it. Hence, man is part of the landscape and knows his place in it. He knows what the mountains mean, and he knows their names. Sacred space is constructed through a prolonged period of orientation. . . . In sacred space, man tends to be at home, at rest, more concerned with being than doing."

   On p. 8 of the same essay, I define *profane space* as "implying a territory in which man believes he has all privileges and no responsibilities. It is homogeneous and neutral, hence without any enduring experiences of qualitative difference. Profane space appears and disappears as a result of expediency and necessity. It is a space to pass through more than a space to call home. In profane space, man feels a profound discontinuity between internal and external reality, and confronted with that discontinuity over a period of time, man is emptied of himself and confronts absolute 'other.' In profane space, things have no names, or only the most general names. In it, man is an alien, an orphan, a wanderer, a stranger; he belongs nowhere and must keep moving to get somewhere but when asked, he does not know where that somewhere is. Man does not know what the mountains mean or their names. It is a spiritless world and all is relative in it. In part, it produces what has been described in Peter Berger's book, *The Homeless Mind* (New York: Vintage Books, 1973)."

7. See Aldous Huxley, "Wordsworth in the Tropics," in *Do What You Will* (London: Chatto and Windus, 1929), pp. 113-129.

8. Joaquin Miller, *Songs of the Sierras* (New York: Putnam, 1923), p. 147.

9. Joaquin Miller, "The Great Emerald Land," in *Oregon*, edited by John B. Horner (Corvallis: The *Gazette Times* Press, 1919), p. 389.

10. *On the Oregon Trail*, edited by Kenneth A. Spaulding (Norman: University of Oklahoma Press, 1953), p. 109.

11. Ian G. Barbour, editor, *Western Man and Environmental Ethics* (Reading, Mass.: Addison-Wesley, 1973) provides an introductory discussion of this *mythos* and the debate about it.

12. See H. L. Davis, "The Old Fashioned Land—Eastern Oregon," in *The Frontier*, 9 (March 1929), 201. Davis comments further about the classic pastoral in confrontation with the western experience: "The nearest approach to Vergil's conception of the trade was a little, falsetto-voiced runt I met once in the Blue Mountains, who lent me his library. It was the complete works of Zane Grey. And he wasn't a good sheepherder, either. His flock was always counting in about thirty or forty short. Vergil's shepherds may not have had more than that many woolies to bother with, all told. An Eastern Oregon sheepherder has charge of 1,000 head, often more. No wonder he can't find time to cut pastorals on the back of trees. If there were any trees to cut them on."

13. Colonel E. Hofer, "Western Literary Militancy," *The Lariat*, 2 (Feb. 1924), 43.

14. H. G. Merriam, "Editorial," *The Frontier*, 8 (Nov. 1927), 1.

15. H. L. Davis and James Stevens, *Status Rerum: A Manifesto, Upon the Present Condition of Northwestern Literature* (The Dalles, Oregon: privately printed, 1927), p. 1.

16. James Stevens, "The Northwest Takes to Poesy," *The American Mercury*, 16 (Jan. 1929), 68. (I am indebted to Professor Glen Love for drawing this article to my attention.)

17. H. L. Davis, *Proud Riders and Other Poems* (New York: Harper and Brothers, 1942), p. 14.

18. Davis, p. 29.

19. Theodore Roethke, *The Collected Poems of Theodore Roethke* (Garden City, N.Y.: Doubleday, 1966), p. 4.

20. Roethke, p. 13.

21. William Stafford, "Having Become a Writer: Some Reflections," in *Northwest Review*, 13, No. 3 (1973), 90-91.

22. John Haislip, "The Example of Theodore Roethke," in *Northwest Review*, 14, No. 3 (1975), 14-20; and Richard Hugo, "Stray Thoughts on Roethke and Teaching," *American Poetry Review*, 3, No. 1 (1974), 50-51.

23. Roethke, p. 202.

24. Davis, p. 33.

25. John Frohlicher, "Philipsburg," in *Northwest Verse*, ed. H. G. Merriam (Caldwell, Idaho: Caxton Printers, 1931), p. 140.

26. Glenn Hughes, "Rain on Orcas," in *Northwest Verse*, p. 196.

27. I propose that David Wagoner is even conscious of this tradition, as he shows in the restraint of "The Poets Agree To Be Quiet By The Swamp," and in the vocabulary of "The Words." See his *Collected Poems 1956-1976* (Bloomington: Indiana University Press, 1976), pp. 20, 53, 67.

28. William Stafford, "Starting With Little Things," in *Northwest Review*, 13, No. 3 (1973), 83.

29. William Stafford, *The Rescued Year* (New York: Harper and Row, 1966), p. 65.

Report from East of the Mountains

Don't say much.
This close to Hell's Canyon
the rimrocks want quiet

so Nez Perce dead can sleep.
Your mouth is dust all August
when the barn roof shines

so steep you must look away.
This is the vast interior now
where fallow ground mumbles

"leave us alone." So be empty
enough to wonder into ponderosa
wild enough to kiss Narcissa

Whitman's ghost wavering across
swales and flats of wheat.
The populous wet coast?

You won't see that trench again.
Alkali and sage hens take you
basalt remakes your fencing hands,

your eyes trace magpies on
rivers of east wind. So be remote.
Visitors may never see this

lost range you settled for—
juniper, mule deer, appaloosa,
buckaroo, riata, Chinese gold.

One Umatilla is your friend.
High blue day on high blue day
the hidden spring gives up its

cold artesian calm. This water
keeps you close to shade, to bones.
By ravenous deserted towns

you are small as a gnat's ear.
At night by an obsidian sky
singing surrounds you—

deep, fragile, far. With such edges
you can let the center go.
The world starts here and is whole.

Coyote Teaches Jesus a New Word

They were going along the Blue Mountains in deep snow. Jesus kept falling through the crust up to his waist, but Coyote was singing and dancing along the top. Jesus was getting mad at Coyote, so he said: "I'll bet you can't even melt this snow." So Coyote said: "Watch. I will do it." He thought a word and the snow melted. Then he laughed and ran up the ridge onto the snow again, leaving Jesus to flounder in the drifts.

All morning, Jesus tried to get Coyote to say that magic word out loud. Coyote got tired and said, "O.K., I'll teach you the word if you promise not to say it too much." Jesus promised. So Old Man Coyote taught Jesus the Indian word *chinook*. "As many times as you say it, snow will melt in a warm wind that many days, but never say it more than three times," Coyote said.

Jesus laughed. "Chinook, chinook, chinook, chinook," he said, took another breath and said, "chinook, chinook, chinook," and he kept laughing and saying it over and over. Pretty soon, the creeks started to roar, the rivers overflowed, the valleys flooded. Jesus was so happy he had learned a new word that wasn't in the Bible. He was going crazy.

Pretty soon, Jesus started to melt too. His white robe and skin melted right into the ground. Coyote looked around for him a while, but there wasn't even a bone left. "Oh well, I warned him," Coyote said. "How did I know he would go too far?"

This is why there are so many bad floods now in the spring. This is why they had to make two hundred dams on the Columbia River. White people all over the low country know Jesus is up there in those mountains again. They know he is saying "chinook, chinook, chinook" but they can't make him stop. All they can say is "Jesus" or "Jesus Christ" when the high water comes.

Translated from *A Snake Trickster Cycle.*

Fence Post Talks

Nothing holds us together
but staples and tension
some stiff chunks of alphabet
at the corners.

Our job is acting afraid
to make exceptions, even
for the shadow of that bull
who might need range.

Split up, shrunk, stuck
in high-paid holes, we wear
old moss caps, pay our dues
to the prevailing weather

and hope the dream deer
will come again tonight
and go easily over
this taut barbaric wire.

❧

Part V

仙 人 掌

你爱郁金香
我爱仙人掌

生长在热带
沙漠是故乡

挺在风沙里
出奇的顽强

那怕再干旱
花照样开放

养在窗台上
梦想着海洋

Cactus

You favor tulips?
I'm for that cactus

Raised in the desert
Town with no address

Sandstorm in its face
All spines still, intense

If it's dry as bones
It carries on, blooms

Feeds on window sills
Dreams of journeys, seas

冰　雹

混进暴风雨里
躲在乌云后面

象漫天的蝗虫
带着厮杀的叫喊

和闪电一起
和雷声一起

突然地来了
突然地去了

它所留下的
是灾难的记忆

光秃的树枝
碎了的窗玻璃

暗了的街灯
人的咒骂和叹息

Hail

Hides inside a storm
Hangs out with thunderheads

Like gangs of grasshoppers
Yells wrack and blood

Gets with the blitz
Gets with heavy rumbling

Hits fast
Pulls out quick

What's left
A real nightmare

Beat limbs
Busted glass all over

Shot-out streetlights
Everyone cussing, moaning

〰

Opening in the Wall
A Note on Collaborative Translation

Everyone was gone. The ten-foot wall around the Foreign Experts Compound was darkening with January rain. Pierre Trudeau, a French-Canadian instructor who'd come to China expecting girls, martial arts, exotic medicines, had broken contract and left for Montreal. His *wu shu* teacher had been arrested at the main gate and his off-campus friends had been interrogated by police. My wife, Elizabeth, had retreated to Australia with our two children after living inside the compound since August. Our children, rumored by "the leaders" to be a "corrupting Western influence," learned to climb the wall after all Chinese students were prohibited from visiting them inside our compound. My colleague, John Moe from Los Angeles, had gone to Beijing with his wife for Spring Festival. I was the only *weigreren* left in Changsha Railway Institute.

Huge puddles formed below me on the cement slabs. Just beyond the wall, sheets of Hunan winter rain staggered across the empty basketball courts. All the students had left for vacation except those few—was I one of them now?—who lived too far away to go and return in the three-week holiday. Rope-wrapped magnolia bowed and writhed in the wet northwest wind. I could see the wavering, dripping gatehouse light, its cord lashing back and forth. Below its white blear, the rain washed like watery shingles down the darkening stucco sides of the gatehouse where

Gatekeeper Chang lived behind the iron bars of his first floor windows. I shrugged, shivered, pivoted my crutches away from the clear cold window. My breath had fogged the pane for a moment, then disappeared.

Inside the heatless cement room, the Hunan winter damp refrigerated the blue walls. Standing my crutches together by my small table, I lifted the quilt draped over it, pulled up my bamboo chair, and eased myself down. At least there was warmth there—an electric hotplate under the table glowed a steady orange grin. It was small. It was illegal. It could burn my socks off. But if I dressed in all the clothes I owned and sat still, that hotplate warmed my shins, feet, and legs to near comfort. My left knee, still healing from a basketball injury, throbbed at the sudden change in heat. I shivered, found my pen, and picked up a new page of these translations begun during those long solitary days.

Before me, a draft of "Fish Fossil." The poem embodied Ai Qing's twenty years of exile from Beijing in the remote, primitive wastes of Xinjiang—China's Siberia. As I read, I began to feel I knew what he meant by "Slow, obscure hardening to death," though I sometimes felt less like a fossil than a kind of confined foreign beast, like the lion in the Changsha zoo who lay soaking in cold rain day after day. And Ai Qing's twenty years of forced exile and state-enforced silence made me feel foolish and humble. I'd only taught at Changsha Railway Institute for six months. Still, despite all Chinese efforts, I wasn't at home. Sometimes, the feeling was somewhere between house arrest and parole. Even though I was assured that the wall, the locks, and the regulations were all for my protection, the room felt like a cell, a tomb. Yet once focused on the poem before me, a cup of boiled water steaming on the stone shelf above the table, I could sit and work for hours and forget the sentence I seemed to be serving by serving the sentences before me. Outside, it was darker now. The rain fell hard and sometimes drove against the glass. I turned on the small desk lamp and kept working that last stanza.

At 7:00, a loud rattle of glass and wood echoed up the stairs to my cement room. In the dark, a strange voice called my name.

That could only be my collaborator, the Dean of Foreign Languages. He'd come to deliver his new drafts and to review mine, as we'd agreed last week. Hesitating at the possibility of leaving the heated table, I heaved myself up and gimped down the frozen stairs to unlock the front door and there—Professor Lu Pei Wu: a sudden round smile, a proud Cantonese head, a long and quickly stolid face, a gray bulk of cotton clothing. He happily clutched his black plastic bookbag under one arm, shook off his rain-drenched umbrella, then came in and began to ask questions: had I eaten dinner, how was my health, had I heard from my family, would I come to his home to make *jiaodza* tomorrow and stay for Spring Festival dinner? I accepted. Gladly. He must have gotten the Party's permission.

He'd come to consider himself my friend, mostly because he alone held enough social position to visit me without fear of Party criticism. While he was not a Party member, he did have good basic English skills learned as a boy in the Yale-China school in Changsha in the 1930s, and those skills had now lifted him beyond the fear of even the new rules which suddenly appeared at the steel compound gates in December: no visitors after 10:00 p.m.; no entrance except on business; all visitors must register at the gatehouse. Professor Lu and I agreed to work together on these translations, he from an interest in English poetry and I from an interest in getting outside the Foreign Expert's Compound and into contemporary China and Chinese literature.

That effort to discover China without the pleasure dome effect created by guides, hotels, museums, friendship stores would not be easy. The Chinese prefer to define, absolutely, a visitor's experience. This creates the false impression that China is a kind of human wilderness dotted with proper places for air-conditioned busses to stop so that a proper number of westerners can get out, eat, spend their money, sleep, and get back on the busses again—a new version of Shangri-La. I'd seen and heard about those cliches. I wasn't a tourist. I was determined to engage the China beyond that utopian, rationalized, commercial structure. Translating, I could perhaps pass through to more authentic experience. Professor

Lu became my guide, then, though he, too, seemed to censor himself quite carefully, afraid—as many Chinese are—of being a source of information about the authentic China of daily life as lived by the Chinese. Of course, I was warned that his interests were not exclusively literary. He really just wanted my help in going abroad to study. I nodded, admitting to myself that my motives weren't purely literary either. I wanted an education in China, genuine China, and I was trying to stay alive.

So sitting in the cement living room, warmed slightly by a coal stove that gave off more monoxide than heat, we sat down and began an evening's work together. Professor Lu took out his thin, ricepaper copies of his translation—word by word and an English version of his own—and unpacked his brick-sized British English/Chinese dictionary, and a borrowed book he'd wrapped in brown paper, *Songs for Coming Home* by Ai Qing. Little by little, as we worked through a reading aloud, then a study of the visual poem, I could feel my throat begin to go raw, my eyes begin to feel heavy, my voice begin to drop octaves. Before I passed out, I'd get up and go to the kitchen, take a lot of deep breaths, then bring back some porcelain cups, a bamboo tea caddy, a thermos of boiled water. (On the coldest nights, we tried shots of Chinese brandy the flavor of old kerosene.) Then, refreshed (the monoxide didn't seem to bother Professor Lu), we'd go through more questions about the meaning of the poem, its lines, its images, its feeling. Inevitably, we'd end our evening by discussing his interest in studying abroad. Shortly before 10:00 p.m., we walked to the steel gate together where he stepped through the steel door and disappeared. He walked carefully, but with a dancer's gait. His hands were fleshy, soft, uncalloused. He could sing beautifully. He wrote poetry. He wanted our children to be friends, but they weren't allowed to visit. Nevertheless, our meetings continued like this—usually reviewing one of my new versions and one of his translations each week.

Some of our meetings were difficult for both of us. Once, I spent a week translating "Ocean and Tears" only to discover that the last word in Professor Lu's translation, *sweet*, had been misspelled as *sweat*. That cost a week of work and put me on edge. I'm sure that some of my gestures also caused Professor Lu equally strained moments. He often looked in vain for my American usage in his British dictionary, and my use of colloquial or idiomatic speech seemed to frustrate him. Yet he was always helpful, controlled, and congenial. We could laugh together. I could surprise him with a line. He taught me Chinese, history, geography, poetry, imagery, mythology, folklore, and even manners. Eventually, I came to believe that because he'd just finished translating a British dictionary into Chinese, he held his translations in higher regard than he actually admitted, and couldn't easily accept my revisions of his work. Could I always say to him that he'd gotten across the denotative meaning but left the poetry behind? So we spent hours checking and cross-checking my versions, he insisting on certain changes, me trying to explain the inexplicable. I wasn't sympathetic to his view of poetry as a simple kind of rationalism devoid of greater suggestiveness and imaginative leaping. As a linguist, he seemed to want clarity, logic, and precision. The last line of "Cactus" was a mystery to him. I didn't want things too clear and explicit. I held out for nuance, implication, suggestion. The last line of "Cactus" was easy for me to accept. Taken together, I suppose we both knew that literalism and free rendition were both inferior forms of translation. So we worked on together, assuming, perhaps intuitively, that our dialogue over Ai Qing might be productive if we could both contain ourselves.

Of course, that description doesn't fully inform. A concrete instance, "Fish Fossil," might better show the nature of our process. Agreeing first on line length and end-rhyme, we talked our way to content very quickly. In the fifth stanza, Professor Lu gave me the following version:

You were absolutely still
You had no reaction at all to external world
(You) could not see the sky and water
Could not hear the sound of the spray.

While this remained consistent with the Chinese original in literal meaning, it clearly lacked a feeling of English rhythm, an emotional movement basic to poetry. So we began our dialogue. From that original, I offered him a draft. He checked it, he asked questions, I answered, I asked questions, he answered, I revised, he explained, I revised again. Sometimes, we went through as many as ten drafts over a period of weeks before we were both satisfied that our interests weren't being neglected. In my final version of that fifth stanza, I rendered it thus:

You're all inert
Your give and taking gone
No vision for sky or wave
An ear for surf left? None.

Professor Lu was satisfied with this, although the faulty parallel in the second line bothered him. It bothered me too, but not enough to give up the rhythm. I hoped Ai Qing would approve.

Other points in our dialogue about "Fish Fossil" included my repetition—not in the original—of *petrified* in the fourth stanza; my use of the noun, *federal assayer,* in the third stanza; my choice of *arrested movement* in the sixth stanza. In the last instance, Professor Lu wanted a word that did not connote *police, crime,* and *legality,* yet I had a good hunch that the poem embodied feelings about Ai Qing's twenty years of officially sponsored exile and silence in Xinjiang, then his sudden excavation and return to the display cases of literary Beijing.

In the last stanza, the problem of literalism was even more acute. As prepared by Professor Lu, the literal Chinese meaning read as follows:

When living, (we) should struggle
In the struggle (we) go forward,
Even to die
We should use up all (our) energy.

I felt this language as prosaic fragments in English, and I could also sense that the feeling in the stanza was clearly affirmation contrasted with the death described in the earlier stanzas. So we talked. We looked at my versions. We talked. I revised. Finally, I decided that the stanza, to hold any concrete feeling in English, would have to move away from bald statement toward image. Also, the tight syllabic structure of the Chinese stanza would require few English syllables and tight music to preserve the feeling of the original language. As finally drafted, the stanza read:

The living need to strive
To act, to move, go on
Then die
Like candlefish who burn, burn.

Professor Lu argued that the *candlefish* (not in his dictionary) image violated the original poem's intention to end with abstract statement. I admitted that *candlefish* was a denotative risk, but I wanted to take it. My collaborator could still be angry. At the time, he was very polite, always polite, perhaps too polite to be true.

So while Professor Lu traveled half of China on school business and administered the Foreign Languages Department, and while I taught sixty senior students of English both writing and literature, we still managed to talk, write, and revise our way through these fifteen translations. When my wife, Elizabeth, returned from Australia in June to see me through a long convalescence after a winter siege with bronchitis, dysentery, and the stresses of isolation, my collaborator and I were just finishing the footnotes and introductory essay for the Chinese version of this manuscript. On the last July evening, I handed over the completed manuscript to Professor Lu and crashed on the berth of a northbound express.

On a July morning in Beijing, I watched my steadfast interpreter, Xu Rei Fang, nervously bounce on the balls of his feet and flip his plastic notebook from palm to sweaty palm. In Ai Qing's hotel room, I watched the old poet—dressed in soft blue shirt, gray slacks—as he stared at Xu suspiciously, then asked his name and work unit. The phone jangled—someone from the Railway Ministry for Mr. Xu Rei Fang. When he hung up, his identity assured, Ai Qing seemed to relax and so did my nervous interpreter.

Beginning our interview I felt an immediate sense of distinction in Ai Qing's face and head. Large, almost square forehead, a heavy shock of irrepressible black hair receding to a deep cove on his right side, his eyebrows canted askew—one dark and thick and curving down normally, the other thin, rising, and fading into flight. I knew he'd been through three wars, feasted at the banquet of political approval, embraced the revolution, fallen into exile, traveled the world, and published more than thirty books—a major voice in Chinese poetry. Now seventy-two, again favored by the state, he seemed a compelling presence. It was as though a center of gravity were concentrated in him, as though all the hope and despair of the socialist revolt were present in that one mind balanced above his soft blue collar and narrow shoulders.

As Ai Qing talked, he smoked continuously. When he opened his wrist and hand and laid them in his lap—as he often did to punctuate his answer to a question—his gestures were made with lentitudinous calm. Sometimes, his wife, Gao Ying, would suddenly and boldly answer for him. She seemed impatient with his silence, his hesitation, his slow contemplative hands. After she spoke, he would lean forward, his hands coming together on his cigarette, and add a few sentences in a soft, low voice. He didn't look at our interpreter. In one silence, he reached out slowly through his haze of cigarette smoke, took my forearm and held it for a moment, as though there was something in me he wanted to touch directly.

Around the hotel room, I could see a few of the objects he admired and often wrote about—two small cactus, large white seashells, dark heavy fossils in gray sandstone. "So much of life—like politics—is soft," he said. "I like what is hard." I saw stacks and stacks of unbound manuscripts on the desks. Were these the accumulated work of the exile? No. All were lost.

Finally, I pointed to one pile on the floor. They turned out to be twenty-five theses on his poetry written by students at Hangzhou. He was supposed to read them and choose the best for presentation at a symposium on his work this year. He shook his head. He wasn't interested in becoming the object of critical industry but that fate seemed inevitable now. Even his recently cast bronze bust displayed on a low shelf in front of us suggested that Ai Qing was bound for display, a symbol of the new arts policy of Deng Xiao Ping. Out the open window behind him, a hammer clanged incessantly on steel.

When we finished the interview, we went to the elevator and waited, noting bricks, mortar, sand, rubble—the continuous construction, destruction, and reconstruction that is contemporary China. Outside, we took a few pictures together. He held steady then, our arms wrapped together, our separate hands holding the Beijing morning. Behind us, nameless flowers bloomed. Before us, the street blared on. The sky, sullied gray, carried on to Outer Mongolia, to Paris, to Oregon, to Changsha. Saying goodbye to him, I sensed that here, finally, was the man whose poems, whose life, had been my greatest opening in a maze of walls.

This is more than I should say about him.

鱼 化 石

动作多么活泼，
精力多么旺盛，
在浪花里跳跃，
在大海里浮沉：

不幸遇到火山爆发，；
也可能是地震，
你失去了自由，
被埋进了灰尘；

过了多少亿年，
地质勘探队员，
在岩层里发现你，
依然栩栩如生。

Fish Fossil

The way you darted
The way you leaped, shimmering
From swell to swell
Free to dive deep or swim

Then, bad luck. The volcano
Ground swell? Some upheaval boomed
Your play and flash all smothered
In evolutionary ash—your tomb

Billions of years later
A new federal assayer hammered
Found you, life-like as ever
In some remote dark stratum

But you're hushed now
Not even a breath
Scales and fins all perfect
Petrified, petrified

You're all inert
Your give and taking gone
No vision for sky or wave
An ear for surf left? None

但你是沉默的，
连叹息也没有，
鳞和鳍都完整，
却不能动弹；

你绝对的静止，
对外界毫无反应，
看不见天和水，
听不见浪花的声音。

* *

凝视着一片化石，
傻瓜也得到教训：
离开了运动，
就没有生命。

活着就要斗争，
在斗争中前进，
即使死亡，
能量也要发挥干净。

Staring at just one piece of you
Any numbskull can see that
Arrested movement means
Slow obscure hardening to death

The living need to strive
To act, to move, go on
Then die
Like candlefish who burn, burn

失 去 的 岁 月

不象丢失的包袱
可以到失物招领处找得回来，
失去的岁月
甚至不知丢失在什么地方——
有的是零零星星地消失的，
有的丢失了十年二十年，
有的丢失在喧闹的城市，
有的丢失在遥远的荒原，
有的是人潮汹涌的车站，
有的是冷冷清清的小油灯下面；
丢失了的不象是纸片，可以拣起来，
倒更象一碗水泼到地面
被晒干了，看不到一点影子；

The Lost Years

Not like losing a bundle
Waiting at the lost and found
Lost years
Can't find where they went—
Disappeared bit by bit
Lost twenty years ago
Lost in hubbub cities
Lost on far empty steppes
In rush hour stations
By lone kerosene lanterns
Lost years
Aren't scattered pages you may gather
More like water poured on loess
Dried—not even a stain left
Time's stream
Can't be dredged or seined
Time's never solidified
If fossilized, it could

时间是流动的液体——
用筛子、用网，都打捞不起；
时间不可能变成固体，
要成了化石就好了，
即使几万年也能在岩层里找见。
时间也象是气体，
象急驰的列车头上冒出的烟！
失去了的岁月好象一个朋友，
断掉了联系，经受了一些苦难，
忽然得到了消息：说他
早已离开了人间

一九七九年八月二十二日　哈尔滨

Centuries later, be a shape in rock
Time's all evanescence
Like smoke from a driven train
Lost years
Are like a friend
Who suffered. You lost touch
Suddenly, news from somewhere comes:
He's long long gone

Notes

Cactus—The poem embodies the poet's affection for flowers and for cactus in particular. It also suggests the fierce or passive exterior—two means of self-protection in China. The poem was written before 1957, and discussing its context caused Ai Qing to recall the large collection of cactus which he enjoyed before being forced into exile. Rather than abandon the plants, he gave them to a Beijing kindergarten. He hoped to find new cactus in the desert in Xinjiang, but found none.

Hail—Written during his exile in Xinjiang, this poem describes public destruction created by the hail of warring street gangs during the civil war which is usually called the Cultural Revolution. The diction is more formal in Chinese.

Fish Fossil—This poem was written after the fall of the Gang of Four when Ai Qing was again allowed to return to Beijing. Actual date of composition is 1977. The poem describes metaphorically the causes and effects of his twenty years of exile from literary life, during which he was allowed to write but not to publish.
line 8: *petrified, petrified,* not repeated in the original, is doubled here
        for ambiguity and rhythmic integrity of the line
line 20: *candlefish* is a species of smelt burned for light by certain
        American Indian tribes on the northwest coast.

Lost Years—Written in 1978 during a visit to Harbin, this poem was prepared for an audience who gathered to hear Ai Qing speak about his twenty years of suffering exile and silence. Instead of making a speech, he wrote this poem and read it. In conversation, he said he preferred this poem to many others in the book. "That time was gone forever," he said, "and the poem should be sad."
line 11: *lost years* is isolated here for emphasis and tension in English.
        This change from the Chinese original also apears in line 22.
line 13: *loess* is a buff to yellowish-brown loamy soil found in North
        China and elsewhere. It is believed to be chiefly deposited by
        wind. This word is used here for *ground* becuase it is homo-
        phonic with *loss.*

Part VI

Sooner or Later, Something's Got to—

Well, I was lined up behind this old woman in a gray coat at the checkstand. Ahead of us there was this fat woman in a purple and white snowmobile suit. She was hunched over waiting to write whatever the checker said, no problem. My mouth started to water when I saw she had every kind of meat, wine, and cheese you could think of and a great big frozen turkey. Like to know where she gets that kind of dough. The old lady in the gray coat leaned over by her ear.

"Doesn't look like anybody's starving at your place, eh?" Her voice was raspy and loud like she was part deaf. Everybody started gawking at us. The kid punching the register stopped for a minute. The box boy smiled a little, but he was too cool to laugh. I couldn't believe an old woman would say something like that right out. Made me feel good. Then she leaned over again.

"How about I come along to your place for supper tonight?" The purple and white snowmobile suit was flustered, gave her a hot stare, then tried to stare at the cash register. Her hair was piled on her head like some kind of black haystack.

"That's $76.25," the checker said. "Will that be all today?"

The woman didn't say anything, just scribbled out the check and walked away like a plowhorse. I almost laughed, I was feeling so good. I usually don't like standing in line. The kid started to total up the old lady's cat food and gelatin.

"You charged me too much for the cat food. It's on sale," she said. The checker's face turned red. I almost laughed again. He looked at the cans and told her the price again in a smartass voice. Makes you want to give him a lick. The old lady said no, so he flipped through the pages of his price book, dropped his pen, bent over to get it and banged his head on the cash drawer. I had to look away. You could cut the air with a knife. The old woman didn't say anything, just signed the refund amount, then paid for the cat food and gelatin from her black coin purse with the little crossed snaps on top of it—$1.56. My Grandma used to have a purse like that.

"If prices don't go down pretty soon, I guess I'll have to start stealing some of this stuff. Got my cats at home, you know, and they have to eat too." She looked at the kid as she spoke. Loose skin sagging down on her throat and working back and forth, a flowered scarf tied under her chin. The kid was red-faced, had a white dent on his forehead that wasn't quite bleeding. You could see his ears were burning.

"There's nothing I can do about that, mam." He ripped off the ticket and threw it in the sack.

"Your store, isn't it? Mark the stuff down."

"I just work here. Why don't you buy the dry food? It's cheaper."

"Humf. My cats wouldn't touch that stuff. My son is coming home next week for Thanksgiving. He'll know what to do." She started away and the box boy asked if he could help her put the sack in her car. "Here, give me that fool sack," she said. She took it from him with a quick jerk and walked away, limping a little to one side, the hem of her coat swaying back and forth. I could see her dark nylons rolled down to just above the knees and she had on some dirty white shoes like nurses wear that were split out at the corns and run over on the side she favored. I watched which way she went while the kid totaled up my cottage cheese, liver, and bananas. I gave him a food stamp. "Have a good day," he said. They all sound the same. They say the same thing every time to everybody. You know they don't mean it, like the little button they wear—"Since we're neighbors, let's be friends." What a crock. I don't know any of those people. They're not doing me any favors, I'll tell you that. Everything is supposed to sound like a bargain, but that's all. And you're supposed to pretend it is. I didn't answer the checker. I just picked up my groceries and left. Too much of that supermarket talk starts to burn me after a while.

Outside the wind caught me, made me take a big breath. I always like to get out of those automatic doors. A freezing rain was melting on the hood of my old Chevy. Off toward Broadway, I could see the old woman pushing her little two-wheeled wire cart toward the corner light. Pickup started fine this time.

"You like a ride?" I hollered at her. The pickup was idling too high and my muffler was almost shot. I shoved my chains and sawbar over on the seat and pulled the gas can over out of the footspace. The old lady looked up at me like she heard, so I hollered again. "Want a ride?" I saw her face then, dark pouches under her eyes, wrinkled skin drawn tight on her cheeks. Looked like my Grandma before she died. "No thanks, son. Maybe another time," and she started off down the walk. What you going to do? Can't say I didn't try. I slammed the door and drove up to the corner. Light was red. Probably scared the old lady half to death. I watched her in my mirror as she bumped along the sidewalk. The rain was freezing on her scarf, making it shine in the streetlight. All of a sudden, she stopped, looked around, then unbuttoned her coat and reached inside her dress like you see a woman do if her strap falls off her shoulder. She lifted out something kind of red and shiny, dropped it in her sack in the cart. She reached in again and took out another one of whatever it was. Looked in the mirror like a heart when you're butchering at night. The light changed and I drove off, thinking about that old lady. By god, I had to admire her. I don't know what that stuff was, but she sure knew what she was doing.

Nights like this I always take my time driving home. First thing when I come in my wife's going to ask, "Did you get a job?" and I say, no, I didn't get no damn job. I tell her to go look herself. Everybody's out of work, seems like. That's the way it goes. Bigbutt down at the Employment Agency says I should go back to school, get another skill, and move again. Well, I moved seventeen times in seven years and I ain't moving again. Been working in the woods so long now I don't know what else I'd do. So they laid me off. What you going to do? Can't go out and make somebody give me a job fallin' or buckin'. You just got to sit and wait. Don't chew your nails, that's what Jack says. Don't see any collectors hanging around tonight. Sometimes they park down the block and wait by Jack's place. Maybe I better drive around once more. You got to be careful. Better take those green discount tags off the liver too. Wife sees those, she has one hell of a fit.

After dinner I saw the lights on out in Jack's shop so I went over to see what he was up to. Smells like old oil-soaked planks. Jack's working on his pickup just like everybody else. Man out of work with no wheels is in bad shape. That's what Jack always says. He turned around from his workbench and gave me that come-on-over look so I walked over to watch him. Jack doesn't say much, just kind of whistles and talks to himself while he works. I told him about the old lady at the supermarket and he liked the story. Said she still has her pride anyway. They can't take that away from her. He kept scrubbing away on some valve covers, but the solvent was dirty. Jack never buys any. He just waits for it to settle out, then uses it again. Smart man, Jack. I learned some things from him.

"What you got in those crocks?" I pointed over toward the stove. Jack gave me a weasel look like he'd been on the midnight requisition again. He picked up a rag and wiped his hands. "Got to let those soak some more. Come on."

We walked over to the tan crocks behind the stove. I never saw them before. Jack took the top off and said, "Smell that," so I bent over. It smelled sour with something like a little tobacco sack floating in it. "Beer," Jack said, and made that little whistle when he breathes. "You and me will have to bottle it around Christmas." Then he laughed and went over to the stove to stoke it up.

"I never knew you knew how to make beer," I said. Jack sat down on the old nail keg where he always sits and I pulled up a box.

"Man can make most anything if he has to," Jack said. I nodded. Good feeling in Jack's shop; fire going, parts and stuff and good tools, lots of good tools. Sometimes I wish I could live here. Jack's even got himself a little cot over there in the corner. He comes out here, takes forty winks now and then. Jack didn't say anything, just kind of stared off through the rafters like he was looking right through the roof, so I asked him what he's doing Thanksgiving.

"Don't know, Glen. Hadn't give it a thought."

"Let's go shoot a goose. I got a couple shells for my gun."

Jack tipped back on his nail keg, gave me a big laugh so his gums showed. "You can't shoot no goose now. Where you going to shoot one?"

"Out the refuge," I said. "One shot will do it."

"You better stick to your bow."

"I been watching a spot where they come in every night."

"Ya, but who's been watching you? Those Fish and Game guys watch that place like hawks."

"I go out just after dark, see. Scatter a little corn for a few nights." And I told him about how I had it figured, but I could see he didn't like the idea of poaching a goose with a gun. He shook himself back and forth on the keg. He's a big man, Jack is, and quick as a bear. He said he'd rather go hungry than go to jail, so I said I'd get the goose and he said he'd bring something, maybe a pumpkin pie or something. He grew lots of pumpkins. We sat around for a while chewing the rag about one thing and another, then he went over to his little frig and took out a couple of cold beers. Jack is a good man. We talked some more, fire died down. Jack stoked it up again with some of that good tamarack we cut this fall. Jack didn't get his deer. I saw a buck but missed him. Track soup. Well, I told him I better be getting home, so he locked up and turned out the lights except for a heat lamp he had rigged on the beer. I walked on home. So cold the snow squeaked under my boots. That's one thing, by god. I got a good pair of boots. The stars are up there so far away I don't know what to do. I started to whistle and first thing some mutt starts barking at me so I shut up. Think I'll stay up late tonight and watch TV. They might pick it up in the morning; you never know when they're coming.

It was still snowing when I got up and had some coffee; wife's gone back to bed, kids gone to school now. Jack's gone some place too, least his pickup is gone. I see old Hopkins still hasn't taken the wood heater out of his trailer like the city told him. I didn't think he would but you never know. I can't see why he has to take it out myself, but the city said to take it out or move out of town. Always pushing somebody around. Frankie Younger's going out to rustle some beef tonight. I think this is the night. Fresh meat for Thanksgiving. He wanted me to go along too. I can remember we used to have steak and eggs for breakfast on the farm sometimes. Old Gramp sitting around talking about the Depression and how he used to eat oatmeal mush three times a day. Least they have food stamps now. Better go down and sign up again. I hate this living off the government but what else you going to do? I ain't proud. I got a wife and two kids to feed. So what else is new? Maybe I should go with Frankie. They said they got a couple of steers all staked out up in the timber. Nobody will ever catch them. They're positive. Maybe I better go over and see those guys again, see if they're still going. Have to siphon a little gas some place tonight, can see that right now. Jack says we're like Robin Hoods in reverse; take it from the rich and give it to ourselves. But you gotta choose careful; not everybody can lose a gallon of gas. God, a piece of bacon would taste good now; even the smell would do me for a while.

Pulled into Frankie's driveway and all his skinny hounds came out barking. Don't know how he feeds all those sons of bitches, honest I don't. He must do a lot more poaching than I know about. I waited in my pickup until Frankie came out in his undershirt, don't dare get. He gave the hounds a shout and they all scattered and shut up. I rolled down my window part way. Frankie had a butcher knife and a steel in his hands, just swishing that knife back and forth over the steel. I don't know how he can stand the cold.

"Well, whatta ya say, Robin Hood? Got your bow and arrow ready?" Frankie laughed and his chew showed brown along his gums. He stopped sharpening his knife and ran his thumb over the edge of the blade. "Feel that!" he said and held out the butcher knife to me. I rolled down my window a little more and ran my finger over the blade sideways.

"Feels good, Frankie, feels good. You getting ready?"

"We leave about six tonight. You coming? I said to Fred the other day, I bet a buck Glen will come too. He's starting to look hungry."

"Well, I been thinking about it some more . . ." I looked at Frankie slipping that knife back and forth. He scared me the way he looked when he did that. He was fat, and the cold made his skin red. Fred had the freezer all empty. I had the bow. Bow's fast and quiet if you shoot good. Easy to get up close to a cow too. We had it all talked out; each man gets a quarter. I get a hindquarter for doing the shooting. "You think we still ought to do it?"

Frankie just looked at his knife some more and kept sharpening it to a fine feather. He was a good fast butcher, wouldn't take him twenty minutes to gut a steer. He looked up at me, his face all full of marks and said, "Well, Robin Hood, what's the deal?"

"Jesus, Frank, I don't want to get caught. Jessie and them got caught last year. I'd rather go hungry than go to jail. Least I still have my pride that way." Frankie's looking at my pickup.

"I bet this knife goes right through that tire slick as a whistle. What you say, Robin Hood?" I stepped on the gas a little and started to roll up my window some. Getting cold in the cab.

"Mitch has a bow. He told me he wanted to go if I didn't. I gotta take off."

"Sure, sure. We'll let you know how the steaks taste." He went back in the house and all the hounds came back barking their fool heads off and jumping on the running board again. I thought for a minute I was going to get stuck in the driveway. I was spinning, but I rocked back and forth a few times and made it out backwards. Chevy's a good pickup long as you put a little weight in the back end in the winter. This year I threw in some big tamarack chunks Jack cut. They did the trick.

Must have been about 4:30. I was on my way home when I decided to swing into the supermarket just to see what they put on discount today. I was grabbing a cart when I saw the old lady in the gray coat again. Pushed my cart along behind her to the bakery counter. The girl came out of the back room.

"Can I help you?" she said to the old lady. The old lady took three or four of those doughnut samples on top of the counter and ate them like she was getting ready to buy some.

"No thanks, dearie. Everything looks so stale tonight." She limped along the glass cases in her gray coat without even looking at the cookies and cupcakes. I have to look at them myself, even though I can't buy any.

"Can I help you?" Same brass voice the bakery girl used on the old lady. She used it on me before too. Means "What you gonna buy?" That girl always looked like a chicken to me, the way her face was so red and narrow lips. I said no thanks and started to follow the old woman when the bakery girl leaned over the counter. "See that old woman? Every time she comes in here, she eats a handful of those samples and never buys a thing."

"Maybe she's hungry," I said, trying not to look at the samples myself.

"And you know what else? Always says the same thing about everything being stale. Next time I'll put the tray away. That'll fix the old biddy." She laughed again, almost like a chicken, I swear. I pushed my cart away and nodded at her. Can't take much of people like her. The old lady was almost to the cheese case at the end of the aisle when I saw her again. I was looking past her and kind of daydreaming when I saw them. You would miss them if you weren't looking right at the spot. There were some eyes and a nose just above the stack of eggs. Somebody was watching. The old woman didn't see them, I'm sure. She was picking up one of those red round cheeses and I couldn't see what she did with it because her back was to me. She looked around at me and I started to read some labels and she turned sideways and picked up another cheese and now I saw her slip it inside the top of her coat. I looked at the space between the eggs where the eyes had been. They were gone, and the old lady had rolled her cart around the corner, still nothing in it. I could hear her huffing down the aisle on the other side of the food shelf. She was just about opposite me; you could hear her breathing. I heard the soft metal tearing—a can tab opening—and a slurp, then some fast drinking, then the rattle of an empty. Overhead I saw the sign for fruit juice. Grapefruit juice, I bet. This old lady knew what she was doing—by god, she did. She must be on Social Security.

I picked up some discount cottage cheese and, just as I was rolling away, the metal doors at the end of the dairy case swung open with a bang and a short bald man in a green apron came out walking like he was headed some place important. I rolled my cart up where I could watch him. He went right to the manager's little office and they nodded and pointed and watched the aisle where the old lady was coming out now, still nothing in her cart. The whole store was hung with bright paper turkeys. Big stacks of cranberry sauce and juice were piled at the end of aisles. I watched them to see if they were going to put the squeeze on her then, but they let her walk right past. Get her when she goes out. I wheeled my cart toward the bananas, trying not to listen to the supermarket music. I always look for the black ones off in a cart by themselves and marked down to maybe five cents a pound. They want you to buy them in bunches, but I cull out the rotten ones. Clerks give me the eye when I do it, but it doesn't bother me any more. They can't make you buy the rotten ones if you don't want to.

I was just cutting around this corner on my way to the checkstand when the old lady in the gray coat came around the corner too. Wisp of gray hair thawing on her forehead.

"Now look here, young man. I want to show you something." She turned her cart around and led me back to the aisle she'd just come from. "Just look at that." She pointed at the shelf. "This package is pure gelatin. No sugar or flavoring. That one is 45 cents more and all it has is a little raspberry and some sugar. Isn't that something?" She looked up at me like I was supposed to know exactly what to say. All I could think of was the cheeses she had stashed away. She had a big mole, almost like a wart, on one cheek and some black hairs sprouting around it. "My doctor says I have a condition. I'm supposed to drink two packages of this every night with a little honey. Sleep like a baby."

"You ever try these bananas?" I pointed in my sack. "They're really cheap."

She leaned over and looked in the sack in my cart. "Those are rotten."

"No they're not. Just dead ripe."

She put her nose back in the sack, then stood up again and made a face. "Smell rotten to me. I wouldn't eat them if you paid me. Why don't you try some of this?" She took a package of gelatin off the shelf and dropped it in my cart like she owned the place. I really didn't need the gelatin, but I didn't want to hurt the old lady either. I was having my doubts about telling her, couldn't think of a way to say it, so I just gave up and said it right out.

"Listen, they saw you take the cheeses." She looked at me like I'd said something she didn't quite hear. We just stood there. I could see the manager watching us.

"You'll have to speak up," she said, putting her hand to her ear.

"They saw you take the cheeses. There was somebody behind the eggs. You better put them back." She turned and started to walk away from me, almost like she'd never talked to me. Her slip was showing a little below the gray coat. When she turned the corner at the other end of the aisle, I turned around and crossed in front of the manager, skipped the housewares aisle and went down the animal food aisle where the old lady was standing by the cat food. I pulled up next to her, trying to act natural about everything. That's what Jack always says, act natural. I could see the manager fiddling around with some stuff at the other end of the aisle. The old lady was putting cans of Puss and Boots in her cart with the gelatin box that had the picture of the cow on it.

"Listen to me, old lady. They're up there waiting to arrest you. They know you took the cheeses." She just kept putting cans of cat food in her cart. I was getting hot now. God, she was big. Didn't act afraid of anything. I could see her sitting in the slammer. I been there once or twice myself and it's no place for an old lady. Besides, who would feed her cats? I grabbed her old gray coat and gave it a shake. "Don't you hear me, for Chrissake?" She turned around very slow and looked at me. Her eyes were small and blue-gray, a little glassy. I could hardly look at her face.

"Are you accusing me of stealing?" Her scarf flapped a little.

"I saw you do it. The cheeses are right in there." I nodded at her breasts and tried to smile.

"My son is coming home Thanksgiving. If you keep this up, I'll have to tell him." She put more cat food in her cart.

"Look," I said. "I don't give a damn who your son is. They know you took the cheese, that's all." I pointed at her breast again. "I'll give you some food stamps if you need them." She started to push her cart away so I grabbed the front and stopped her. What else could I do? She gave it a jerk and the cat food started rattling around like hell. I looked up and the manager and a box boy were coming down the aisle at us. I let go quick and squatted by the dog food pretending to read some labels.

"What seems to be the trouble here?" The manager looked at me and then at the old lady. I wanted to lay one right alongside his ear. He knew what was up, I swear. The old lady had her nose in the air like she'd been insulted. She wasn't going to say anything.

"Nothing," I said. "Carts stuck together, but I've got them loose." I stood up and wheeled mine around and rolled it toward the meat case. I heard the old lady ask the manager why the cat food wasn't on sale this week and how did he expect her to feed her cats and have enough for Thanksgiving. I didn't hear what he said, the supermarket music was too loud. But you know what they always say, "There's nothing I can do about it."

At the meat case I watched while a few people came up and stared at the packages, kind of mumbling to each other, maybe picking up a roast, then putting it down, then picking up some chicken wings at the far end. Make a little soup or something, I guess. I found a roast marked *reduced for quick sale* so I threw it in the cart and headed for the checkstand. I could hear loud voices over the music and when I got there a lot of people were standing around watching.

They had the old lady trapped in the middle checkout slot by the scales. The manager was bent over, his arms spread on either side of the chrome bars like a fighter and the box boy was doing the same thing behind her. Manager was red in the face and the old lady kept saying, "Don't you touch me, you beast," and something else I couldn't quite hear about her son. The manager tried to take her by one coatsleeve and the box boy reached out for the other one, but she just shook them off like a hen ruffling her feathers. A lot of people were standing around watching. One man in a good coat came out of the crowd and waved a $5 bill at the manager like a flag, but the manager shook his head and reached for the old lady again. This time he grabbed her under one arm and started to pull her toward the office. Box boy grabbed the other. They had her walked about halfway to the office when the sergeant came in the automatic doors all brass buttons and badges and flags and guns and bullets and black leather. The old lady saw him and collapsed, her arms suddenly falling up around her head. The cop ran over and helped the manager and the box boy lay her down on her coat and they put a sack of sugar under her head. A lady checker came over and pulled her dress down, you could see her stockings in little rolls just above her knees. Her eyes were closed and her false teeth were kind of falling out. She looked bigger and bigger to me laying there and somebody started to unbutton her coat and the red cheeses kind of slid out. The manager picked them up, handed them to the box boy who took them back to the dairy case. The supermarket music kept playing all the time.

I paid for my stuff and started to leave. Damn good thing I didn't have to stand in line. When I was walking out, I heard a big crash behind me, a watery sound. Somebody ran into one of those cranberry juice displays. I could see the juice coming down the aisle. Outside, the ambulance was just pulling in all lights and sirens. I got the hell out of there. A place like that makes me feel like a big tick's sucking on me somewhere I just can't quite see. I'll tell Jack about this, see what he says. Maybe I ought to go with Frankie tonight. I can shoot better than Mitch. I just don't know, by god, I just don't know. Sooner or later—something's got to give or—

Blue Hour: Grandview Cemetery

Three miles out, I die down in grass
guessing here I might be alone enough
to lie and stare an hour. Home is far.
Beside me, black Sancho dog holds his breath
then runs off—cocked after something

articulate with the possibilities of night.
Six ridges away, I hear wildfire burns
driven by hot wind, fought by 800 men.
Today, I watched boys with .22's
killing gophers, as I once did, for fun.

Across the valley, smoke is towering
like a god from fields of grass
burning for the sake of purity, they say.
Why am I so cool and easy now? Still,
alone, cradling my head in my hands

considering evenly
the scream of killdeer over fallow ground
my own yellowjacket sting
the millionaire next door
my jilted neighbor who gave herself away

Venus brighter above the ridge,
I remember the sign at the gate:
NO LOITERING, GUNS, OR ANIMALS ALLOWED.

So let them arrest me. Come on, sheriff.
Find me if you can. I'm guilty, I know,
I must be guilty of too much peace
too many inviolate hours of just lying
on my back in the grass out of town.

I whistle through my teeth. I laugh.
I wait. Here comes that old black shepherd
stinking of skunk to break me out of
this bony wilderness of graves where
for an hour, I was modern, criminal, free—

stealing space for one more groundless prayer.

Nard Jones, Weston, and Oregon Detour

Introduction

One January day in 1978, as students were bundling up to leave my Western Literature class, a girl who always sat in the back row approached me at the lectern. She asked me if I'd heard of a writer called Nard Jones and could she read one of his books for a paper due in three weeks. I didn't know this student well. She was a freshman. She'd done C work in the course so far. She'd been absent a time or two. I asked her which book she was interested in.

"Well, there's this one that people keep stealing from the library at home," she said. I thought I saw a kind of gleam in her eye. I must have looked doubtful. "Really, it's true," she said.

"Where's home?" I asked.

"Weston. Over by Walla Walla," she said and pointed northwest.

"Which book is it that people steal?" I asked.

"I don't know. My mother's got a copy, I think. She's friends with the librarian."

"You grew up there?" I asked.

"Twelve years," she said.

"Well, it should make an interesting paper. Find out as much as you can. Talk to the librarian. Let me know if I can help."

"Oh, good," she said, and I'm still sure she went out with a great smile on her face, as though something about her life was suddenly worthy after all.

That was my introduction to *Oregon Detour*, Nard Jones's first novel and the first "New Realist" novel written in the Northwest. The student did read the book and wrote her paper, but her project raised more questions than it answered. For instance, she said that the author had been run out of town, that he'd been sued, that he'd written an awful book about the town's good people, and that everyone stole the novel. As I read this, something in me began to doubt. Was something being left out? I started to wonder how I might verify any of this.

To begin, I looked through my own research files for a survey of libraries in Eastern Oregon I'd done in 1973, to find what the librarian of Weston had, indeed, said in response to my question: "In your judgment, who are the most important authors who've written about Eastern Oregon?" The Weston librarian had replied:

DeVoto. Probably best known. Parkman. I think Nard Jones progressed into a good writer . . . I can't think of any more really important ones.

Given the student's paper, this was strange. I looked through the librarian's responses for more information. She had listed all of Jones's regional works except *Oregon Detour*. Something *was* being left out. That began to bother me. I'd clearly invited her at numerous places in the three-page questionnaire to mention any fiction about the region.

The more I thought about that apparent omission and the student's paper, the more I wanted to find out what had actually happened. To support that research interest, I wrote a grant proposal to the Oregon Committee for the Humanities, and they generously funded the project for the summer of 1981. To prepare myself for interviews in Weston about the novel, I read ten years of the town paper, the *Weston Leader*, and I dug into Nard

Jones's literary past for weeks with the help of librarians at Eastern Oregon State College, Whitman, Umatilla County, and the University of Washington. With the help of Jones's sister, Audrey Jones Baker, his son, Blair, his second wife, Anne Mynar Jones, and his daughter, Debbie Jones, as well as the honest assistance of Margaret Sutherland, Weston librarian for the past thirty years, and the cooperation of more than 35 residents of the area who granted me interviews— with all of their help, I was able to complete an intensive research project in a six-month period.

That summary does leave out some notable facts: the specific hospitality of Cliff Price, George Gottfried, Hugh Gilland, Wayne O'Hara, and Willmarth Reynaud—Weston people who treated me kindly as a wanderer; the wild-eyed fanatic who walked into the Umatilla County Library in Pendleton and said to the librarian, "You're not fooling God with this library and all your books," then stomped out as I drew the only local copies—non-circulating— of *Oregon Detour* closer to me; my two-year search for a copy of the novel that was rewarded in the Green Dolphin in Portland one rainy night; the immediate sources of affection that sustained me: food brought morning, noon, and night by loving hands, the doe at the spring in the mountain dusk, the generous fertile country where I found wild strawberries . . .

I presented what follows at Concordia College, Umatilla County Library, and at the Pendleton Rendezvous, but the project really culminated for me when, one April afternoon in 1983, I stood before the assembled student body of Weston-McEwen High School in Athena, the school Jones himself would have attended if he were growing up in Weston today. Waiting in that shining gymnasium for silence, I reviewed my notes and watched the energy and excitement in the bleachers turn to attention. I hoped I was ready. For about half an hour, I told them the *Oregon Detour* story as I'd been able to find it. At the end of my talk, I read them part of a chapter about high school seniors from Weston going to Pendleton after graduation for a night on the town. The bleachers began to whistle and cheer. I stopped reading, looked up, waited, then read a few more sentences. They laughed. I read on, stopping while they responded, then reading on again. They loved it. Only when the bell jangled at the end of the day did they let me stop. Busses were coming, cars waiting.

On my way out, the principal stopped me in the front hall. He was a big man who'd gone to school locally and returned to teach. "Nothing's changed," he said. "That part you read? I did that too. These kids will do it too. It's all still the same. Even graduation." As he spoke, students were streaming by with coats and books and packs—voices rich, magnificent, and opening to the spring outside. I hoped there was another novelist among them. At least, I thought, they now have heard that writing fiction was a possibility—even here. At best, if I'd done my work well enough, *Oregon Detour* might again be included as a worthy interpretation of its generative community.

I

Among writers who grew up in the Northwest between the world wars, Nard Jones (1904-1972) cast himself a complex career as a full-time journalist who also wrote seventeen books, published more than three hundred stories in popular magazines, and broadcast numerous radio programs. He published twelve novels, including his national bestseller, *Swift Flows the River*, *Evergreen Land*, a history of Washington, and *The Pacific Northwest*, a regional history co-authored with Stewart Holbrook and Roderick Haig-Brown. Still selling at the Whitman National Monument is Jones's popular history of the Whitman Mission, *The Great Command*. As a journalist, Jones edited for Miller-Freeman trade publications in Seattle and New York for nearly 24 years, then went to work for the *Seattle Post-Intelligencer* in 1953, where he held various editorial posts, including chief editorial writer, until his retirement in 1970. *Seattle*, a history and memoir, appeared posthumously in 1972 from Doubleday.[1]

While Jones's writing still waits for major critical attention,[2] his first novel, *Oregon Detour*, remains important as the first novel by a Northwest writer to use the aesthetics of the "New Realism" established by Sherwood Anderson, Sinclair Lewis, and Scott Fitzgerald a decade earlier. *Oregon Detour* is further distinguished because it has been the object of fifty years of censorship in Weston, Oregon, where Jones lived from 1919 to 1927. Like other New Realist novels across the country, from Hergersheimer's *Cytherea* banned from his hometown library in West Chester, Pennsylvania, to Lawrence's *Women in Love* banned by New York Customs officials, to *Elmer Gantry* by Sinclair Lewis banned in Boston by the local D.A.—not to mention a host of others—Nard Jones's first novel has been frequently stolen from the Weston Public Library, banned from the library shelves, and removed from the Weston High School Library. This essay attempts to document and examine the history of *Oregon Detour*, now an unknown novel.

II

After graduating from Whitman College in 1926 with highest honors in English, Nard Jones returned to Weston, Oregon, to live with his family and to work in the family general store. During that year at home, he continued the literary career he had started at Whitman. He wrote fifteen stories for the popular pulp magazines, a New York market he had been quick to understand. He also wrote weekly editorials for the *Weston Leader*'s publisher, Clark Wood,[3] who was also Jones's literary mentor. Jones's weekly columns showed the major literary influences of his Whitman education: the polemic style of H. L. Mencken, the New Realism of Sinclair Lewis, and the small town interests of Sherwood Anderson.

Also, during that year at home, Nard Jones began to work on *Oregon Detour*, a project he'd started at Whitman when he learned from Professor Russell Blankenship that a realistic novel in the manner of *Main Street* had not been written about any Northwest community.

In September 1927, Jones moved to Seattle to work on two Miller-Freeman trade publications, *Pacific Motorboat* and *Western Woodworker*. In a sense, returning to Seattle was going home. He'd been born in that city in 1904 and had lived there for the first thirteen years of his life, a time when he had enjoyed great personal freedom because his family had owned a hotel there. Now, after eleven years away—California, Eastern Washington, Eastern Oregon—he returned as a fast-rising magazine writer, recent college graduate, new editor, and budding novelist. He moved into a hotel, edited for Miller-Freeman during the day and, bolstered by shots[4] of whiskey which could make him dangerous, wrote *Oregon Detour* and short stories during the evenings. In June 1928, he married Elizabeth Dunphy, the daughter of Walla Walla's leading lawyer and member of a wheat-ranching pioneer family. In March 1929, he hired Brandt and Brandt, literary agents in New York, and sent off the *Oregon Detour* manuscript. Within fifteen days, his new agent had sold the book to Payson and Clarke for $500 plus 10 percent royalties to $5,000, 15 percent thereafter.[5]

Here, then, was a Northwest literary boomer. At 25, he was a veteran of print, a quick learner, a skilled amateur actor with a taste for whiskey, jokes, and self-dramatization. Short, dark-haired, quick, handsome, slender, ambitious, Jones was a compelling presence. To complete this picture of sudden success—comparable to none in the region—all Nard Jones needed to hear was the comment of William Rose Benet, Assistant Editor of *Saturday Review* and Payson and Clarke's chief editor: "Your book seems to be one of the most promising first novels that I have read in some time."[6] After some correspondence between Benet and Jones about revisions, Jones's novel went to press and was released in early 1930. From coast to coast, *Oregon Detour* quickly attracted critical approval.

In Weston, Oregon, however, events had progressed toward publication somewhat differently. Clark Wood, the *Weston Leader*'s publisher, had been trying for nine months to prepare the Weston audience for his protege's novel. Wood had published a letter from Jones in April 1929, in which Jones wrote:

> The hero of this book is the harvest. And any of my friends who circulate the rumor that any of its people are such-and-such persons will be shot in cold blood—even though I have to do it myself. This will take months of time, as I am the most damnable shot in the eleven Western states (April 19, 1929).

In October 1929, Wood had reprinted a complimentary national review of the novel containing the statement that "There is no bitterness in the book. No sarcasm. In writing of his people, the author has not forsaken them." Just before the novel was released, Wood further noted that "Weston is [the] locale but characters are fictitious." This evidence suggests that both Wood and Jones knew controversy was rising like thunderheads over Weston Mountain.

On January 17, 1930, *Oregon Detour* went on sale in the local drugstore, just a few yards from Jones's home on Water Street. (His father was mayor of Weston, a leading businessman, and an avid community booster.) All copies of the first shipment sold immediately for $2.50 each. Those who couldn't afford to buy the novel rented a copy from friends at 25¢ and read it. The Weston librarian, Josephine Godwin, another of Jones's literary mentors, added the book to the public library. It was immediately checked out by a family friend, then by the doctor's wife who read the novel aloud to her husband at bedtime. They laughed over each page and considered the novel a "boy's look at his hometown." Many of the surrounding wheat farmers who did business with the Jones and Jones Mercantile also bought copies of the novel. They felt it was a good-humored use of risque local events. Some snickered that the pious now appeared only sanctimonious. Young married couples in the community—Jones's peers—were especially anxious to read the novel because the word quickly spread that *Oregon Detour* contained "real people."[7]

Nevertheless, a segment of Weston's six hundred people were furious. They were reading *Oregon Detour* as reporting. They called the novel vulgar. They objected to its "hard-talking sloppy lingo," and to Jones's use of names like Fanny Breast and Rev. Alfred Horliss. They objected to his explicit use of sexuality. Those who protested were generally members of two socially powerful groups in Weston, the Methodist Church and the Saturday Afternoon Club, both dominated by socially prominent women who held formidable powers over cultural life in the community. For instance, the Saturday Afternoon Club gave monthly literary programs, reviewed proper books, encouraged musical events, controlled the library board, and at one time owned both the city park—which they later sold—and the local community hall. Their membership was by invitation only.

According to Nard Jones's sister, who was still living with her family in Weston when the novel appeared, a Saturday Afternoon Club member approached her on the street. As she recalled the encounter,

> This woman said, I'm not sure what her words were, but it was something like she thought it was terrible that Nard might have put people in Weston into his book. I remember I was so shocked. I was fifteen, I guess, and I turned around to her and I said, "Mrs. _____, I really think that people must feel terribly important to think that they're in somebody's novel." I turned around and walked away.[8]

Many women in this group refused to read the novel after they heard about its characters and language. It was publicly stated to this writer that there was also a mass book burning to rid Weston of *Oregon Detour*. It was also suggested that somewhere in a Weston attic lies a trunkful of copies waiting to be discovered.

Even though he lived several hundred miles away, Nard Jones immediately felt the tremors of outrage created by his novel in Weston. His response, published by Clark Wood in the January 24 edition of the *Weston Leader*, is worth reprinting here in its entirety as the only document of its kind in Northwest literature—a New Realist asking his subject community to read their lives as literature rather than as reporting:

It's Only Fiction

To whom it may concern: It has been brought to my attention that individuals are looking upon certain passages in *Oregon Detour* as reflective of truth. This is regrettable and far from the real purpose of the author.

Only three actual names appear in this volume: they are merely mentioned in one or two sentences and this mention is intended as a compliment. All other characters are fictional, though necessitating common names which would naturally be duplicated in this and thousands of other books and communities.

It is perhaps needless to say that what happens in "Creston" may happen in a hundred other wheat towns. It is also needless to say that the writer would not intentionally speak in a derogatory manner of those toward whom he has the highest regard.

Authors are frequently confronted with this situation, and it is no new thing. I am sure that the great majority of my home town people will read the book purely as a story, not attempting to weave into it any information which happens to be in their own minds—but which was not in the mind of the author as he wrote.

Very truly yours,
Nard Jones

Apparently, Jones's effort to encourage his Weston audience to accept his fictional masque did not succeed. In Weston, the novel was read in 1930 and is still read today as "about Weston" by the majority of residents. Trying to figure out or trying to remember who the "real people" were in the novel is still a local pastime. There is no evidence that the novel was ever understood as literature, as a statement by Jones that Northwest small town life is—at best—a dangerous idyll.

Biographical evidence also suggests that *It's Only Fiction* was as much a feigned professional pose as it was an effort to claim his innocent intentions. Jones was not afraid of controversy. In fact, he sought it. At Whitman College, he scandalized the campus his senior year by writing and publishing an underground sheet called *Spasm*. His editorship of *Blue Moon,* the campus literary magazine he founded, was constantly under challenge for publishing "blue" literature rather than writing of the "sunny side." His *Weston Leader* columns were often pure provocation. Thus, the professional innocence projected here only conceals a part of Jones that was iconoclastic.

However, other evidence suggests that Jones was not invulnerable to the snarl of the Weston status quo. Most significant in this respect must have been his now lost letter to Clark Wood in April 1930, to which Wood responded as follows:

Dear Nard:

Have no regrets about your novel. It was a good yarn—the proof being that I was absorbed in it myself when usually I don't care a damn about anything except a detective story with a mysterious murder in the first chapter—preferably a double murder.

The sex stuff naturally caused some comment around here, but they ate it up. Those who didn't buy the book, borrowed it. I realized that you had to put in this sort of stuff in order to sell the yarn and I thought you handled it with extreme skill.

Some of the descriptive work—notably the flood and the wheat harvest—was strongly done, and was almost as good as yours truly could have evolved.

Forget it, boy. You haven't lost any real friends around this burg.

Woodsy

April 16, 1930[9]

The tone of Wood's letter suggests that Jones needed to be reassured about his potential loss of popularity at home. Evidently, behind the young New Realist's mask lived a writer both sentimental and nostalgic about Weston—a town where he'd actually been given the impetus to become a writer, a town he would visit annually for most of his life, a town where he gave copies of his books to the library, a town he wrote about in both fiction and journalism for the rest of his career.[10] Private sources also confirm that Jones himself was "very, very shy . . . he was not a daring person." He hated flying and avoided autograph parties as much as possible.[11] Even though he could call on national reviews, Clark Wood, and New Realism to shield him, a part of Jones was still vulnerable to the possibility of local dishonor.

III

Of course, Jones tried to convert this furor into a joke for Northwest writers who read *The Frontier,* the region's leading literary magazine. In the November 1930 issue, Jones reported his recent news in this fashion:

Nard Jones, Seattle, is finishing a second novel, *Sin of Angels,* for spring publication. He has two long stories and a short to *College Life:* "Hollywood," "Expatriates," and "Please May I Have Another?" For the past three years Mr. Jones engaged in trade journal work. Recently he took the *Oregon Detour* by auto—"without being shot at, or hanged."[12]

While levity here worked to preserve some professional dignity, more important adjustments were going on at the typewriter, where Jones had just finished his second novel, *The Petlands,* and was at work on his third, *Wheat Women.* In advance notices for *Wheat Women* published in the *Weston Leader* in November, Jones continued to respond:

I am doing another wheat novel in order to show the other side of the picture depicted in *Oregon Detour.* That book showed many of the faults of the wheat land; this new wheat story will show many of its virtues. It will probably, therefore, be longer.[13]

Is Jones attempting here to recover from what he's decided were his excesses in *Oregon Detour?* Is he playing to an offended audience with tongue in cheek? Is this the final evidence that he himself was unprepared for the implications of his first book? All seem likely. He was also careful to add a disclaimer to the front matter of *The Petlands,* in which he reminded his readers that the "story of this book is fiction."

Subsequent events in Weston allegedly took several turns against Jones and *Oregon Detour,* turns which seem to have been dominated by the Saturday Afternoon Club. Most conspicuous were those hostile moves alleged in the local narrative about *Oregon Detour* recorded by the student writer, namely that Jones was sued and run out of town. There seems to be no base in fact for either of those charges. No evidence of a lawsuit exists in Umatilla County courts or in the memories of more than thirty informants. Also, Jones was clearly not run out of town, since he had lived in Seattle for three years prior to the novel's publication. Further, Jones returned to Weston in June 1930, for a two-week summer vacation with his parents. According to family sources, Jones's father, Nelson Hawk Jones, would never have allowed the young novelist to return for the Pioneer Reunion if there had been any threat of violence against him. Jones also returned to Weston for Christmas that same year, and usually made an annual trip to Weston the rest of his life.

Thus it appears that those who faulted *Oregon Detour* attempted to honor their own opinions by literalizing the novel and defining the novelist as criminal and outcast. In fact, there was never unanimous Weston disapproval of *Oregon Detour*. Jones did not lose his rapport with the majority. There was no suit. There was no expulsion. Even today, Jones's novels can be found in many Weston homes and many Westonites remember him fondly—jokes, boozing, pranks, stories, and favors.

However, the question of the book being banned or stolen from Weston libraries has a factual basis. Shortly after the novel was published, a student at Weston High School gave a book report to his English teacher on *Oregon Detour*. She immediately removed the book from the sophomore reading list and the high school library. Weston Public Library records show that the book was added to the Weston branch in 1930, but soon had to be re-ordered from the main Umatilla County Library in Pendleton. The librarian confirmed that this could only mean the book was no longer in the Weston collection. In 1935, the novel seems to have been restored to the Weston branch collection, but by 1936 *Oregon Detour* again had to be ordered for Weston readers from Pendleton.[14] Evidently the novel was being stolen, a conclusion supported by a retired Umatilla County librarian, who stated that she was told "not to send *Oregon Detour* to Weston because it would never come back." Since the Saturday Afternoon Club still controls the library board in Weston, no copy of *Oregon Detour* has been housed in the Weston Public Library for at least 26 years, the tenure there of the current librarian.

167

This apparent popularity of *Oregon Detour*—as a book to be stolen—is matched by an equally durable outrage about the novel that appeared in various guises during this research. The angry were generally old "native" members of the Saturday Afternoon Club or directly related to them in some way. One interview, for example, contained these comments:

Why you going around trying to get the skeletons out of the closet? Looking for a nigger in the woodpile? I can't see any good in it. I'm not going to tell you anything even if you want me to. I heard you was going around doing this. Why stir people up again over something that happened fifty years ago? You should let well enough alone.[15]

Other members of that group refused to be interviewed. Still others feigned ignorance of the entire event and its consequences, even though they were recommended as highly informed sources. Evidently, the small segment of the community that initially felt it had been slandered by *Oregon Detour* still feels that their reputations have something to lose some 51 years later.

Whatever the causes of their silence, the Saturday Afternoon Club and the women of the Methodist Church have made their judgment about the novel and its censorship a fact of community life. Only *one* opinion about *Oregon Detour*—the Saturday Afternoon Club opinion—seems to circulate in the community. Research at Weston McEwen High School in 1982 revealed that no current students had heard of the novel or read it, and only a few of their parents had heard of the novel at all. The book was not housed in the high school collection even though the high school librarian had heard of the book herself.

Yet banned book status for *Oregon Detour* by the offended minority is qualified. Recently, a farmer on Weston Mountain called Nard Jones's son in Walla Walla and asked if he could still buy a copy of the novel. Also, a woman who'd spent her summers in Weston for forty years finally sought out a copy of the novel in 1982 and read it herself. Her conclusion: the book was tame. Finally, the novel is in demand. Umatilla County Library records show that, between 1937 and 1959, one of two main library copies circulated 22 times for 3 weeks each. Another

Umatilla County Library copy circulated 29 times between 1966 and 1973, including three successful circulations to the Weston branch.[16] Most of the individuals interviewed during this research wanted to know where they could find a copy of the novel, or if there was one in the Weston library. There wasn't. Only two non-circulating copies remain in the main Umatilla County Library in Pendleton, and both are in moderate demand—but must be read in the library. There seems to be a continuing if not increasing readership for *Oregon Detour*—the local classic.

IV

Why all this fear of a book? There are three factors at work here—all very concrete and powerful—which might serve to explain what happened. First, the events and characters in *Oregon Detour* were neither genteel nor romantic, and didn't fit with the formula romances and westerns that dominated popular reading tastes in Weston in 1930. In Chapter II, the new high school teacher, Florence Larson, is discovered upstairs with Swede Mongsen, a college dropout and farmer, in *flagrante delicto* during a moonshine dance at Swede's farm. In Chapter V, Etta Dant, the major point-of-view character, is seduced by her high school boyfriend on graduation night. Believing she is pregnant, Etta and her boyfriend, Charlie Fraser, decide to elope. On their wedding night, Etta discovers that her menses has only been delayed. Peg Nettleship, Etta's girlfriend, is converted to a life of passion by a traveling evangelist. She becomes a wanton about town, and in Chapter II, Part III, Peg is caught in a hotel room in Walla Walla by Swede and flees before his wrath to Etta and Charlie's kitchen wrapped only in her lover's coat. Charlie is finally seduced by Peg also, but their affair ends when Peg falls out of Charlie's car on the way up cemetery hill for a final seduction on the night of the Pioneer Reunion. Such realism in event and character was unprecedented in Northwest fiction, which even caused the novel to be a best seller in Portland for more than two months.

169

Also, whatever he claimed, Nard Jones had actually changed these events and characters very little, and where he did alter events those alterations were not understood by his Weston audience. Adopting New Realism, Jones had written a contemporary pageant without the benefit of historical distance. The only place name Jones changed was Weston, which became "Creston." All other place names—Walla Walla, Pendleton, Portland—remained the same. No common landmarks in the community were renamed, local character names were only slightly altered, e.g., Clark Wood became Clark Tipp, and some local character names were not altered at all—as Jones acknowledged in *It's Only Fiction*. Local traditions and events—a flash flood,[17] the Pioneer Reunion,[18] and high school graduation,[19]—were all basically unaltered. In fact, they were hardly disguised. Where Jones needed plot material, he took it directly from community rumor, public event, or his own experience among his peers—including *all* sexual antics.[20] Thus, suspension of disbelief was impossible for the Weston audience. While Jones's close group may have hoped to see their collective portrait in the novelist's mirror, they didn't expect to see so much of that face—the shadow.

This fracturing of genteel literary expectations by *Oregon Detour* extended itself to become a second cause of uproar and popularity. The community's illusions about itself had been threatened by a New Realist novel—a common event in the decade. As Donald Meinig has noted in *The Great Columbia Plain*, the Weston-Walla Walla area "during the first decades of this century seemed to be overshadowed by the massive influences of a crass materialism, strident boosterism, and a frantic concern to be in the forefront of 'progress'."[21] Like other New Realists, Jones had stripped away Weston's white enamel of piety, progress, and propriety to show local individuals becoming the natural victims of their own ignorance, fear, violence, customs, and self-deceptions. The sons and daughters of the golden pioneers were not only masters of a beautiful landscape; they were also slaves to their inner landscape, especially their sexuality, loneliness, and insecurity.

Third, *Oregon Detour* also reversed community power structure and social privilege, a potent change which Jones himself might not have recognized would occur when he wrote the novel. Suddenly, an "outsider" had exposed the "natives" to the possibility of public censure. In many Northwestern towns, these two social classes are defined by the Oregon Trail experience. The ancestors of the "natives" came overland, homesteaded, founded the community, created its institutions, and commanded its wealth. According to Weston sources, the "natives" did not hold their members up to public censure. In contrast, the "newcomers" were those individuals whose families had settled in the community after 1900. More than likely, the "newcomers" bought land from one of the "natives," or carried on business, services, or other forms of labor. They would not be invited to join the Saturday Afternoon Club, but would form the Fun and Fiction Club. At the Pioneer Reunion, they would not be eligible to nominate the Pioneer Queen. When *Oregon Detour* appeared, the "newcomers" were not threatened, since Jones had taken his major characters largely from "native" wheat families whose lands surrounded "Creston." However, the life beyond reproach that the "natives" enjoyed had been redrawn by some newcomer who'd kept his eyes and ears open. Ironically, it is the outrage of the "natives" that has kept the novel alive in the community.

V

It is obvious that this microcosmic conflict and its causes are not unique. The information here invites the reminder that such conflicts are universal in literature—Flaubert, Steinbeck, Wolfe, and Malamud (after *A New Life*), to name a few. However, in the Northwest this is the first and oldest case of local censorship and of public furor between a novelist and members of his community—perhaps a sign that literary culture had begun to rise from those authentic sources called for by H. L. Davis and James

Stevens in their 1927 Mencken-style polemic, *Status Rerum*.[22] With the single exception of Vardis Fisher's agrarian novel, *Toilers of the Hills* (1928), the modern Northwest novel did not begin to appear before *Oregon Detour* was published. In fact, Northwest novelists whose works are still reprinted and studied today all began to publish their major books after 1930: H. L. Davis, James Stevens, Darcy McNickle, Vardis Fisher, to name a few. Thus, it may be fair to conclude that *Oregon Detour* was the region's first modern novel, certainly the Northwest's first exercise in "New Realism." Now the novel is generally unknown except in a small Eastern Oregon community where it still compels attention.

Notes

1. A Nard Jones bibliography is provided on page 175, but many of these titles are out of print.

2. See the following for brief biographical or critical sources on Nard Jones:
   Lancaster Pollard, "The Pacific Northwest: A Regional Study," *Oregon Historical Quarterly*, LII (September 1951): 226.
   Alfred Powers, *History of Oregon Literature* (Portland: Metropolitan Press, 1935), p. 638.
   Harry R. Warfel, *American Novelists of Today* (New York: American Book Company, 1951), p. 232.
   Who's Who in America (Chicago: Marquis Publishers, 1956), p.1343.
   Jean Cook, *Washington Authors* (Seattle: Washington State Library, 1936), p. 3.

3. See George S. Turnbull, *History of Oregon Newspapers* (Portland: Binfords and Mort, 1939), pp. 326-27, for a sketch of this unique and talented journalist.

4. Interviews with the Jones family confirmed that Jones's use of alcohol, which began at an early age, became a liability to him and his family throughout his career. The shots of whiskey, according to one source, increased to fifths during an evening's writing. Sources confirmed that, when drunk, Jones could become violent, poetic, or both. When he was sober, his sense of humor and compassion returned. His struggle with alcoholism reached its peak in New York in 1952, a fact which eventually caused his family to return to Seattle without him.

5. All biographical information in this and subsequent paragraphs has been gathered from Jones's unpublished papers, Whitman College archives, interviews with the Jones family, the *Weston Leader,* and sources listed in 2 and 4 above.

6. Letter from William Rose Benet, Assistant Editor of *Saturday Review* and Editorial Advisor to Payson and Clark to Nard Jones. New York, April 1, 1929.

7. Evidence in this and subsequent paragraphs was gathered from more than thirty interviews made by the author in the Weston-Walla Walla-Pendleton area between March and July 1981. Because of the controversial nature of this inquiry, all quotations and sources are presented anonymously.

8. Interview with Audrey Jones Baker, Walla Walla, June 3, 1981.

9. Letter from Clark Wood, Editor and Publisher of *Weston Leader*, to Nard Jones, April 16, 1930. Jones's original letter to Clark Wood has been lost, as have the Clark Wood papers.

10. Jones continued to write about Umatilla County people and events throughout his career. His description of the Pioneer Reunion from *Evergreen Land* was republished in *An Anthology of Northwest Writing*, Michael Strelow, ed., (Eugene: Northwest Review Books, 1979).

11. Interview with Audrey Jones Baker, Walla Walla, June 3, 1981.

12. *The Frontier*, 11 (November 1930), 101.

13. *Weston Leader*, November 21, 1930.

14. Unpublished circulation records, Umatilla County Library, Pendleton and Weston Branch Library, Weston, 1930-1959.

15. All informants were guaranteed anonymity.

16. This confirms the continuing absence of the novel in the Weston Branch.

17. A major flash flood swept through Weston on Sunday afternoon, July 1, 1927. It was carefully reported by Clark Wood in the *Weston Leader*'s next issue. Jones included the same flood in *Oregon Detour*, pp. 74-88, but made major changes. In the actual flood, Newt O'Harras' home was completely washed away, but no one was killed. In the novel, the flood kills an innocent woman, Lura Dyer, which causes one of the main characters, Etta Dant, to blaspheme.

18. Jones's description in *Oregon Detour* of the annual Pioneer Reunion was praised by the student writer referred to in the Introduction to this paper for its continuing accuracy. Others, including Clark Wood in the letter cited earlier, have also noted Jones's accuracy in detailing this event. He later included a similar description in his history of Washington, *Evergreen Land*, as noted in 10 above.

19. High school graduation, pp. 100-114 in *Oregon Detour*, was presented to the current high school student body in May 1983 as a brief reading. The nearly unanimous opinion of both students and faculty was that the same atmosphere—right down to expressions on faces—still prevailed, as did the aftermath—a night out in Pendleton.

20. The accuracy of Jones's transcription from his peers' experience was confirmed in numerous interviews. Many informants either

knew or recalled without assistance the individuals in the community who had served Jones as models for Etta Dant, Florence Larson, Peg Nettleship, Swede Mongsen, and Charlie Fraser. Many interviews also confirmed that Jones made composite characters, concentrating separate historical events into one character's experience in the novel.

21. Donald Meinig, *The Great Columbia Plain* (Seattle, University of Washington Press, 1968), p. 511.

22. H. L. Davis and James Stevens, *Status Rerum: A Manifesto, Upon the Present Condition of Northwestern Literature* (The Dalles, Oregon: privately printed, 1927).

A Nard Jones Bibliography

Oregon Detour (realistic novel). New York: Payson and Clarke, 1930

The Petlands (realistic novel). New York: Brewer, Warren and Putnam, 1931

Wheat Women (realistic novel). New York: Duffield and Green, 1933

All Six Were Lovers (realistic novel). New York: Dodd, Mead & Co., 1934

West, Young Man (or *Young Pioneer*) (juvenile novel). Portland: Metropolitan Press, 1937

The Case of the Hanging Lady (mystery novel). New York: Dodd, Mead & Co., 1941

Swift Flows the River (historical novel). New York: Dodd, Mead & Co., 1940

Scarlet Petticoat (historical novel). New York: Dodd, Mead & Co., 1941

Still to the West (realistic novel). New York: Dodd, Mead & Co., 1946

Evergreen Land (state history of Washington). New York: Dodd, Mead & Co., 1947

The Island (realistic novel). New York: William Sloan Associate, 1948

I'll Take What's Mine, (original paperback). New York: Gold Medal Originals, 1955

Ride The Dark Storm (original paperback). New York: Gold Medal Originals, 1955

Driver's Seat (biography of Dave Beck). New York: Doubleday, 1956

The Great Command (or *Marcus Whitman*) (Whitman mission history). Boston: Little, Brown, and Co., 1959

The Pacific Northwest (with Holbrook and Haig-Brown) (regional history). New York: Doubleday, 1963

Seattle (history/memoir of the city). New York: Doubleday, 1972

Writing on the Hill

See them white rocks on the hill?
Some kids did it years ago—
maybe Halloween—I don't remember now.

Cop didn't see a thing, you know.
Next morning, we're all looking—
a real surprise. Good kids around here

and once a year they went up there
to shove the rocks in place, splash
some whitewash on. Made you feel

good, like you really did live
somewhere important for a change—that big
white "B" and nothing else around

for miles but brush and trees. Then,
last year—I suppose you heard—
some kids went up at night, wrote a dirty

word. You could read it twenty miles
away and everybody knew who did it
in a day—I had to laugh to myself—

and a couple high school girls had
to take it down or be expelled from school—
that's what they say. That's kids

for you. They did it four or five times
that year and pretty soon the mayor had
a fit and got the hardware store to give

the high school ten sacks of cement.
You know what happened next. There's
just not much for kids to do

in a town like this, but they find
something, you know, just like we used to.
Now, did I ever tell you about that

time we—

✺

Part VII

Directions for Visitors

If you want to find my place
get out of town any way you can.
Find the Cascades in early morning.
When you see the Tatoosh Peaks
where the Nisqually flows
into Alder Lake at Elbe, stop,
ask directions at the grocery.
I won't be mourning in the tavern.
The Post Office closed last year.
I have no phone and mail hardly comes.

Take the road to Alder by the lake.
When you see the garden above the road
that will be Uncle Ernest's homestead.
He's 95 this year, prays every day.
Keep going. When you reach the crest
you will see Uncle Leonard's pasture
on the left, Grandpa Mayo's honey house
across the road. Grandma still lives
that farm alone. Cross the swamp
on Alder Creek past Uncle Charlie's pond.
My father's house is on the left knoll.
He died and I moved away to town.

On the next wide curve, turn right
onto the gravel going uphill until
you come to a Dead End sign hidden
in the grass and fireweed. Turn there.
To the right. This will be two ruts
a berm of grass down the center
mudpuddles and chuckholes all along.
In one place, a creek flows across.
No more signs now. Curves will be blind.
I'd suggest slowing down.

In two miles, you'll come to a gate.
Park there and get out. You will hear
Clear Creek splashing over stones,
a dipper will welcome you upstream.
Follow the current through bracken
buttercups, devil club, blackberries
skunk cabbage, deadfall cedar and alder
until you come to a waterfall and pool
surrounded by second growth fir.
I should be there fishing somewhere.
You may see the smoke from my fire
rising like a ghost through green limbs.

If you don't see me, don't call.
This place can't hear a shouting voice.
I'll know you have come by the way
the crows and chickadees carry on.
I'll come out then and eat lunch
with you and we can talk and feed sticks
to the fire. If you wait an hour or more
and I don't appear somehow,
I'm simply not the George you knew.

Catch a few fish for yourself then—
under the falls is the best cast.
If my fire's out, there's still wood.
Make a fire of your own, eat, get warm,
and leave the same way you came by dark.
Please do not tell anyone where I live.
Try to forget this place all the way home.

Barn

"How much hay will this one hold?" I asked and swung open the old doors. Inside, I could hear the shapes begin to move, the silence yawn.

～

Call it close place of barley, summer's house, call it stable. Remember the swallow, owl, mouse living inside the word larger than the neatness of furnished rooms. Name the tack room harness—hames, collars, tugs, bridgen, whiffletrees, bridles, bells. Note the granary, its sacks of oats bulging, its old bins and smell of mice. Touch the chewed wood of the manger, the dung-splashed stanchion. Remember the shake roof, its acres of cob-webs draped gray and shaking thick with dust, its chinks of light. Remember the dead flies against the splotched milky glass, the bedding three feet thick and reeking of ammonia. Name the gutter, scoop, cupola, bag balm, hayhook, pitchfork. The words come over the threshold like cattle called "Comeboss, comeboss" ringing their bells through the deep mud trail in the alder woods while other words hide silent in the straw.

～

Outbuilding. Away from the house. Inside, the barn's gray rain-polished boards let in long slats of yellow light where we played wild yelling bootless Kings of the Mountain in the loose hay. I saw the hay dust boiling up toward the rain tapping the cedar shakes above the loft. In that Platonic cave, rich with the odor of cut clover, we climbed the high solid bones of rafters and beams, rode the braced timbers like horses of joy. Somewhere, the quick squeak of mice—a nest of pink thumbs squirming. When the dog barked, we looked out through the unbattened cracks, our hair full of seed, our rioting stilled.

Grandpa and Grandma coming through the pasture swinging the milkpail between them like a silver moon. Suddenly, we were spies whispering over our wooden guns. Sucking her splayed hooves out of muck, the Jersey cow swayed in like a steaming orange-white giant, her hooves thudding the planks, her udder swollen with milk. We watched through the knotholes as Grandpa swung down the three-legged stool, Grandma dumped feed in the manger and called the cow who came forward. Latching the stanchion shut, Grandma talked to the cow until the first milk pinged into the pail, the white foam gradually building on the surface and the ping changing to one-two-one-two low pulsing spurts. Out of nowhere the wild barncats crawled, waiting by the pail until Grandpa aimed a teat of milk, squirting over their faces, the cats licking so fast, so hungry, pawing the sweet air for more, then slinking away. Upstairs, we laughed and heard the cow low. Nothing seemed to be too much in the barn except that sudden hoof in the milk bucket, that sudden swat of a wet tail in the face.

How we learned to say "close the door; were you born in a barn?" I don't know. How we learned to tease the kid throwing snowballs with "you couldn't hit the broad side of a barn" I don't remember, but the kid always threw harder and missed more. And the chubby girl I loved who was "broad as a barn" and the hot-to-trot girl who "lit out of here like a heifer out of the barn"

who probably took too many tumbles in the hay? Where have these come from? Early, somewhere, even before kindergarten, I learned to see the open zipper on my brother's jeans, his flannel shirt stuck out and a flash of white underwear and even now the phrase bolts: "Your barn door's open." There was subtle pleasure in saying a thing that way. For emphasis, we might add "Cows are getting out." Everybody knew what it meant, but something was still spared the unzipped kid; something became laughter that could have been cooped up and unhappy. Once, I said that to an old carpenter at work. He looked down, took hold of his fly, and as he slowly zipped it up, he winked at me and said "No old horse gonna get outta that barn anyway." He laughed as he said that and I laughed too.

"Now up on the home place, at least we had a good barn," Uncle Leonard would say as he lit the match with his thumbnail and sucked the flame down into his pipe. "My father built that barn by hand the third year we moved out from town. I split the skakes after school. That's the only thing I don't like about this place." He paused, blew a mouthful of smoke toward the ceiling, then said: "just a bunch a rundown sheds." I drank coffee and listened. I could tell he didn't even like to say *shed*; it meant an inferior structure—small, weak, inadequate. I guessed then that the high basilica of his father's Dutch barn—the center bay with loose hay mowed to the rafters (under the Jackson fork) and two side alleys for feeding stock—those spaces he carried inside him like a sanctuary.

The first year we built the new barn, swallows with gabled tails swarmed to its fir boards and tacked their mud apartments to the joint between the rafters and the plate under the eaves. In and out all summer they swooped, banked, glided, dove, and mosquitoes disappeared in their wedge-shaped beaks. Resting on wires between the house and barn, twittering constant in the late evening, the slate sheen of their wings would flash any light. For hours, they carried my eyes and ears in and out of their nests where four or five smaller peeping wedges would plug the mud tunnel entrance. In September after the first frost, they would gather by the lake in thousands and, seeing them there, I would feel as though the barn were flying away, as though they were taking it south with them. Then, I would try to make up a song.

In the lower stall one September, I noticed a barn swallow apparently hanging in mid-air. Walking closer, I saw the thin irridescent gleam of fishline. Woven tight into the mud-daubed nest, one dangling loop of leader had caught the swallow's wing and it fluttered there until it died. I left it there—one swallow making a fall.

The cats who came from nowhere and stayed all winter, the mice by the thousands they chased: the barrel of skunks my cousin jumped into one day playing hide and seek; the owls perched in the loft, their heart-shaped faces white as ghosts; the rats who packed all the apples, tinfoil, and nails into their nests; the nights in England I slept out of the rain in English barns; the men who have slept as strangers in our barn; the North Wind robin I memorized early who flew to the barn to keep herself warm and hid her head under her wing: who are we all together here like refugees in a line? Is this barn the wood shape of hope? Nothing so tightly built or locked that some other unknown life can't get in, sleep warm and dry a night or a year and, somehow, wake and go on?

"Never play with matches in the barn," Grandma said. "Rats will light them with their teeth." "If someone wants to sleep in the barn, always ask them if they smoke. If they say yes, don't let them sleep in the barn—no matter what." I saw her do that once. The men promised they wouldn't smoke, but she turned them away to the road again after supper. "We don't want to see the barn burn down," she said. "What would we do then?"

Old Jesse told me once how all the farmers sat in their barns rainy days and just watched out the door. They couldn't stay in the house; the wife would nag them to death. They leaned over a stall and watched the horses snort through the hay. When they raised a barn for neighbors, and all the men and women around worked together for a day, they'd dance that night on the threshing floor in the center and fiddles would winnow and flail until midnight or later. "A bunch of men could build a big barn like that an' they didn't have no architect," he said. "But these here schools, now, they have to pay a bundle just for a damn architect, but when you go inside them schools, what do you find half the time: a big space in the middle and alleys down both sides—just like a barn."

"Out behind the barn" was the locale of emergencies. If two men had a quarrel, they settled it there. If a boy got in trouble, he took his lickin' there. Old Jesse asked me why I was trying to turn back the pages of time, and I said what did it matter if that time was seen solid and clear. Maybe we should live in barns like the Dutch just to keep us loose and imagining more than the human city, I said. I wondered out loud where all the fighting and smoking and screwing around was happening now. Probably down some back alley or in the back seat of a car, Old Jesse said. Even the wild oats gone to town. Give me the squeak of the latch on the stable door, I told him. That's just enough time to get on your clothes and hide in the hay somewhere while your mother calls your name and you can keep on kissing. "George, you come in the house now, wherever you are," that big voice would say.

One summer a swarm of wild bees hung thick, gold, trembling near the ridgepole, slowly surging back and forth over each other—a dangling cluster. Gradually, they began to draw out white slabs of new comb. We left them alone except for the rocks boys will throw on dares before they run from the stinging sure to come. Those bees stayed up there three years. "It's as good thing they're not in the attic," Grandma said. They left one spring in a great swirling swarm, just as they had come. We never could climb high enough to reach that honey in the peak.

His little finger clamped against his right palm told a story. In Wisconsin in the barn one summer, that finger caught in a hay pulley, didn't heal right, never went to town to have it set by a doctor. Grandpa called it his hook and, pulling fingers, he would always match his bent hook against any man's straight one. He said he always won, except the last time he went back to Wisconsin and some husky cousin pulled that little finger straight—the wound opening again. He doused it with mercurochrome and refused to see a doctor. Back west in Washington, he let it heal to his hook and never pulled fingers again.

And how many men found hanging by their own ropes in the barn? And how many girls, how many women, giving birth still to their children in the mother hay? And how many men falling from the timbers, crushed under the weight of grain, kicked by horses in the stalls? And how many calves butchered and hung high to cure, and how many lambs and pigs—all these gone to veal, mutton, bacon? This is the house of blood, breaking water, birth, afterbirth, despair, mistake, meat, death. Yet the newborn calf wobbles slick and wet and does not hesitate to drink.

The green leatherbound diary doesn't show his crippled walk, his arthritic hands on the pitchfork loading the wheelbarrow in the dark barn. These were his record of four days in 1949:

Sunday, June 12: To Sunday S. and Church, Oliver Aus here, got sheep. Mrs. Mayo and boys here, had lunch on lawn. Robert Mc. here in evening.

Monday, June 13: Sharon and Shirley wheeled 90 loads manure. Alice washed dishes. Bible study in eve.

Tuesday, June 14: Cleaned out sheep barn all day. Sharon and Shirley wheeled 100 loads manure. Alice washed dishes. Robert Mc. got hurt in woods.

Wednesday, June 15: Nice day 68-38. Hard wind in afternoon. Sharon and Shirley wheeled 68 loads manure. We finished in forenoon. To Bible study in afternoon. Barn ready for hay now.

These are the names of Alder neighbors and friends to him. I am called "boys," one of those eating on the lawn. Later, I would wheel the barrow for him too, a nickel a load, and count with Uncle Charlie the number of times I rolled down the planks and out the door to the steaming pile.

In my dream, there is a girl leading me by the hand to her barn. Inside, her high swing hangs from the beams by two thick ropes. The seat is wide enough for both of us and we begin to sway and pump our legs easy and rise slowly holding onto each other and the ropes. Swinging higher and higher over the hay, the pits of our stomachs beginning to glow, our faces tighten as we get ready to bail out and fall forever to loose hay loose hay, the swing above us gradually slowly waving over us like a dark pendulous jewel.

～

Eli and I worked together that summer outside Cheney filling the barn with bales. I drove the truck that pulled the wheel loader while Eli balanced on the bed and stacked the load. At the barn, I backed into the dark huge doors and stopped. While I climbed to the top of the stack, Eli started the mechanical stacker and set the bales on and they climbed to me waiting high in the peak sweating like a horse up there close to the metal roof pinging everywhere and baking my head in an oven, the sweat stinging every scratch it could find. Below, Eli stood in one place—calm, old, red-faced, white-haired—drinking water. Watching him from the high stack, I knew suddenly why the work was divided this way. I was young and smart—I thought—but Eli worked in the cool and stood in one place. We piled that hay for four weeks right to the rafters and out the door, me on the hot stack in the barn, and driving, Eli riding the cool truck deck and smiling. At night, before we slept in the sweltering bunkhouse, coyotes and black-spangled sky everywhere, Eli told me about riding trains and sleeping in barns and under bridges all over the country. At a rescue mission, he had to sing an hour for just a doughnut and coffee. I couldn't stay awake to hear all his stories— the kid, the summer hayhand, who pretended not to be a student at all.

～

Will these fit somewhere? The joke Jesse told about the farmer who went crazy in a round barn looking for a corner to piss in; and Uncle Leonard saying as he smoked how, if the barn was larger than the house, you knew the man was boss, even as we sat in his small house surrounded by sheds; and the farmer who went to Portland where he saw the high hotel and asked, "How much hay will it hold?"

The troupe director said actors have been barnstorming since Shakespeare or before; the poet told me to watch for a barn converted into a house near 20th Place; the doctor invited me to play a little barn basketball; the secondhand store owner has his barn filled to the peak with furniture; the magician had his barn packed with books; the evangelist held his revival meetings in a barn outside Seattle; the curator stands in his converted museum; the grocery called the Red Barn stays open later than Safeway: these are some of the possible interiors, the shapes a huge container can contain. These are just a brief beginning.

I think of the ark, the barn Noah built to hold the animals and family two by two, the barn as ship creating the world again. Across the wide stubble, such barns appear to be huge wood ships moored to the fencerows—the rainbow of old wood that men built as covenant with the animals, neighbors, children, gods. Strong enough to hold some huge possibilities through the temporary chaos of flood or winter, then wise enough to let the sheltered all go out again to recreate the world, such structures seem to always be getting built in spite of scoff, despair, doubt. In winter storms, they seem to float.

Is this the modern fear that fixes old barn boards and beams in the houses of cities, that makes the barnboard market great? The ark—that covenant of husbandry, magnanimity, community, regeneration, memory, family—all being lost little by little as we watch the dream of barns disappear in the nightmare of urban boxes thick with only pets? Do we want those barns back, say, one barn for every three blocks, a barn for every school to prevent complete illiteracy, the gable or the gambrel roof that puts the hand of the ancient in every day?

~

"And did you close the doors?" he asked me.

"I left just a crack—enough for the cat to get in," I said. It was dark then, and we went toward the house. Behind me, I felt the barn settle, articulate with weight. We had filled it again. Everything seemed to hold together now by what we didn't say.

~

Forgive Us . . .

Fifty years of your butchering art
are here, Grandfather. I hear the crash
of your falling ax into alder, the whisk
of your keen knife on the blue steel
while lambs and wethers bleat in the barn.

They knew your one quick stroke across
their throats would make their ends
the best you could create. I still don't
like the blood, Grandfather, but I know
now the need for meat.

"Nothing should suffer," you said,
and sought out old dying queens in hives
and pinched their heads. Mensik's calf—
you told us not to watch; bad dreams
would come, you said, so we walked out

and watched you anyway through a crack
in the wall. One deadly swing—no more—
from the spiking maul buckled the calf
instantly to its knees on the hay.
We knew your power then, and ran away.

And now this God, Grandfather, this God
whose songs you sang, whose church
your worship built, whose book you read,
whose name you never said in vain—
He's got you here in His shepherd's barn.

Oh, he's a shoddy butcher, Grandfather.
He's making you suffer his rusty dull
deathknife for years, crippling your legs,
then cutting off your speech to tremble,
then tying you up in a manured bed.

He won't bring you down with any grace
or skill or swift humane strike of steel.
Day after day, you sit in His hallway
in your wheelchair and nurses walk by
like angels and shout half your name.

Ah, this God of yours, Grandfather, this
God has not learned even the most simple
lesson from the country of your hands.
You should have taught him how to hone
His knife, that the slaughtering of rams
is the work of those brave enough to love
a fast deft end.

Sleeping Upstairs

After the kiss, the tucking in
the footsteps down, the light out
always he listens in the night
a boy alone in his attic bed
for late cars sizzling by in rain
sees their brief lights washing
on the strong rafters just overhead.
Warm in soft flannel pajamas
Warm under Grandma's comforters
his hand holding onto a bedpost
he lies awake in the dark.
The sandman comes after prayers.
"If I should die before I wake
I pray the Lord my soul to take,"
was what he had been taught.
What he believes is the sound of
rain on Grandpa's cedar shakes
lulling him, easing him to sleep
the sound of those old voices below
holding him safely there—upstairs.

Credits

The author and publisher gratefully acknowledge permission to reprint the following works:

Poetry Northwest, for "My Mother Is This White Wind Cleaning" first published in Vol. XXII, No. 2, Summer 1981; "Blue Hour: Grandview Cemetery," first published in Vol. XXI, No. 1, Spring 1980; "Forgive Us...," first published in Vol. XIX, No. 2, Summer 1978; "The Trail to School," first published in Vol XXI, No. 1, Spring 1980; and "Voice from Another Wilderness," first published in Vol. XXI, No. 1 Spring 1980.

Oregon Arts Commission for "A Note For Primary Art," first published in *Oregon Arts Commission Newsletter,* Summer, 1979.

National Council of Teachers of English for "Poem Against The First Grade," first published in *College Composition and Communication,* Vol. XXV, May 1974.

CutBank for "Conjuring A Basque Ghost," first published in *CutBank,* Vol. 16, 1980.

University of Washington Press for "Continuity in Northwest Literature," first published in *Northwest Perspectives,* 1979.

Northwest Review for "Hail," (By Ai Qing), and "Fish Fossil," (by Ai Qing), first published in *Northwest Review,* Vol. 22, No. 3, 1984.

Prescott St. Press for "Forgive Us . . . ," and "Directions for Visitors," first published in *Off The Main Road,* 1978.

"Forgive Us..." was also chosen for subsequent inclusion in *Pushcart IV.*

"The First Day of Summer" also appears in *Willow Springs,* number 18, Spring 1987.

"Coyote Teaches Jesus a New Word" also appears in *Ice River,* 1986.